MW00879854

Death in a
Small Town

Death in a
Small Town

Betty L. Alt

Copyright © 2020 by Betty L. Alt.

Library of Congress Control Number:		2020914634
ISBN:	Hardcover	978-1-6641-2305-2
	Softcover	978-1-6641-2304-5
	eBook	978-1-6641-2303-8

All rights reserved. No part of this book may be reproduced or transmitted in any form or by any means, electronic or mechanical, including photocopying, recording, or by any information storage and retrieval system, without permission in writing from the copyright owner.

This is a work of fiction. Names, characters, places and incidents either are the product of the author's imagination or are used fictitiously, and any resemblance to any actual persons, living or dead, events, or locales is entirely coincidental.

Any people depicted in stock imagery provided by Getty Images are models, and such images are being used for illustrative purposes only.
Certain stock imagery © Getty Images.

Print information available on the last page.

Rev. date: 08/07/2020

To order additional copies of this book, contact:
Xlibris
844-714-8691
www.Xlibris.com
Orders@Xlibris.com
813824

The setting for *Death in a Small Town* is a place in Colorado, where I lived or visited during my first twelve years. The creek, the houses, the alleys, the railroad tracks are as I remember them. The Methodist Church still sits at the top of the hill, and the cemeteries are still located near each end of the town. The sheriff is based on a distant relative who was a sheriff and whom I saw occasionally in the early 1930s. Today, all of the people I remember are gone from the small town, and my characters are drawn from those long dead and mostly forgotten.

This book is entirely a work of fiction. As far as I know, no children were murdered in my small town as portrayed during the books' nearly eight-year time line. In my memories, the 1930s were a time when children could roam freely around the small town and wade n the cool water of the creek without any feeling of fear. However, in this tale, dark shadows lurk outside the safety of homes, and the town's children become the victims of a disturbed mind.

The author wishes to thank both Sandra and Chris for the time they spent reading and commenting on the manuscript. Thanks also to the members of my family for their help and patience during the completion of this project.

Look into any man's heart you please, and you will always find, in everyone, at least one black spot which he has to keep concealed.

—Henrik Ibsen, *Pillars of Society, 1877*

As bad luck would have it, the three boys found the body. They had been told to stay away from the creek that ran through the south end of the small town, had even been warned that they would be swallowed up by quicksand and disappear from sight. However, on the hot afternoon of July 1934, the cloudless blue sky, the shade from cottonwood trees lining the creek bank, and the bubbling water was too tempting to ignore.

"What's that over there?" John Bower called to his two friends as he wiggled his toes deeper into the cool sand of the creek bed.

"Over where, J.B.?" Tony Wells responded. "I don't see nothin'. Where you lookin'?"

"I don't see nothin' either," Wells' brother, Toby, responded. He was a year younger than the other two and usually repeated whatever his brother said.

"Under those willows and that other brush. The red color. It looks like a coat. Might be worth something. You two blind? Come on. Let's see what it is."

The three slowly made their way across the creek, careful to keep from stepping in a hole and possibly losing their balance. Although the creek had only a little over twelve inches of water in it during the months of July and August, it was full of small rocks and had an uneven bottom. The boys knew that if they fell on the slippery rocks and got wet, they would have to make certain their clothes were dry before going home. Otherwise, a scolding from their mothers and possibly a heavy swat on the backside from their fathers would be the result.

As they got nearer, they could see that the red color was actually a bundle of something and protruding from it were two legs. "Oh, God,"

J. B. exclaimed, abruptly drawing back and causing Tony Wells nearly to lose his balance.

"What? What is it?" Tony asked.

"It's a person. There's a person lying there. Move back! It's a drowned person," J. B. replied as he waved the other two back into the stream.

"What person?" Tony asked. "Let me see, J.B. Let me see!" He moved around Bower and pulled back a strand of willow branches that partially hid the body. "It's a little girl. Gee! It looks like the little Gower girl . . . you know the new minister's littlest kid. What's her name? Jenny . . . or something like that."

"Let's get out of here! Come on! Right now!" J.B. yelled as he motioned Toby away from the body and back toward the opposite bank. "We're gonna have to tell someone. We've got to tell someone right now."

Reluctantly Tony let go of the branches and followed the other two boys across the creek where the three hurriedly donned the socks and shoes they had carefully placed in the shade of a tree. While they might be in trouble for playing in the creek, they were very aware that they could be in bigger trouble if their shoes were ruined. Money had been scarce during the past three years of the the Depression and although both the Bower and Wells family were lucky enough to have fathers working for the WPA, their small wages barely covered the two households' monthly expenses. J.B. noted a small hole in the sole of one shoe and knew money would need to be available to have it half-soled. A new pair of shoes was out of the question.

"Who we gonna tell, J.B.?" Tony asked.

"Yeh, who we gonna tell?" Toby repeated.

J. B. rubbed his hand across his head, causing an unruly walnut brown curl to tumble into his dark eyes which, no matter what he had done, always had the look of complete innocence. Pushing the hair back, he looked at Tony and his little brother and thought how, except for the small age difference, they could almost be twins. Blonde hair, straight as a ruler and so light it appeared white was plastered to their heads with sweat. Days in the summer sun had scorched their faces and arms to a deep tan, and eyes so faded blue they seemed almost colorless peered anxiously at him. Apparently, the two had given any decision to him, and he knew he had to provide an answer. After all, he was considered the leader of the gang of three and needed to take charge.

"We could go up to the sheriff's office, but I wonder if he would believe us. Might not be anyone there but old Mabel, and she'd call our moms first thing.

We could just go tell my mom and ask her to tell the sheriff."

"That won't work," Tony interrupted. "We'd be in trouble. Even if we said we hadn't been in the creek, she'd see our pants legs are wet. There must be somebody else."

"Well, what about my Aunt Tillie?" J.B. responded. "She'd believe us about the body, and she wouldn't nag us about being at the creek. You guys know my aunt. She'd know what to do."

The other two nodded. Almost everyone in the small town knew J.B.'s aunt. She and Norman Wellsby had eloped to Raton, New Mexico to be married. Raton didn't require a marriage license, and many couples took the Raton route when they decided to tie the knot, especially if parents disapproved of the union. It had been rumored that Tillie was pregnant when she and Norm married; however, their baby girl, Eleanor, called Nellie by family members, was not born until fourteen months after the union which had left the gossips without their usual whispers of forbidden lust.

Frequently, the boys dropped by Tillie's house after school, supposedly to play with the couple's little girl who now was an adorable three-year-old with long blonde curls. The fact that Tillie usually had cookies or a pie in the pantry was not mentioned by anyone.

"Good idea, J.B.," Anthony said, and Toby echoed the sentiment.

Instead of going up Main Street, the boys ran through dusty gravel-strewn alleys for several blocks and then exited on a north street that faced the railroad tracks. The Wellsby house, which the couple rented, sat across from the tracks on a large lot shaded with boxelder trees. It had been built in the late 1890s and showed its age, the front porch sagging a little and its white siding with green trim needing a new coat of paint. Daily, the rumble of coal trains and the one passenger train caused its windows to vibrate and the floors to tremble. Still, the couple felt lucky to be able to afford the house, and Tillie dutifully tended a garden of vegetables, its outer edges a blaze of yellow marigolds and red zinnias. Near a sagging fence grew several large clumps of Bouncing Betties covered in white blossoms. Tillie tolerated them, even though she thought they were weeds, as they delineated her home from a vacant house which had fallen into disrepair years earlier.

Although they had selected Tillie to be the recipient of their news, the boys were hesitant to just blurt it out. For a few minutes they played with the small girl, but Tillie could see that something was amiss.

"What is it? What have you three done now?" She pushed a stray caramel-colored lock of hair off her forehead and looked from one boy to another. Placing a plate of cookies on the table, Tillie admonished them not to get crumbs on her recently laundered table cloth. Then she went to the ice box crammed in a corner of her small back porch to get a pitcher of iced tea. Like most in the town, Tillie's husband made little money working in the nearby coal mines, but the one thing she felt they could afford, actually needed in the summer months, was ice. Three times a week the ice man drove his wagon to their house and always being careful of the dripping block toted it into the ice box.

"Might as well tell me," Tillie insisted as she poured tea into glasses and set one before each boy. "I know you've done something you shouldn't have."

"We've been down at the creek," J. B. began. "We know we shouldn't have gone there, but . . ."

"We found a body," Anthony blurted out. "We found a body!"

"I was telling her," J.B. said angrily as he took a swipe at his friend. "Let me tell her."

"A body," Tillie interrupted. "You found a body? A human body?"

"Well of course it was human," J.B. said, a disgusted look on his face. "If it had been a skunk or coyote, we wouldn't have come here. We came here so you could tell us what to do."

"And so we wouldn't get into trouble with our folks" Toby added.

Tillie Wellsby was stunned. She wasn't certain how she should reply. At first she thought the three were just trying to see how she'd react to their story. However, after a minute looking at all three faces, she could see that the boys were frightened and were being truthful. She also noticed the damp trouser bottoms on all three which confirmed that they had been at the creek. Sweat from running had dampened the hair of the boys and plastered it to their heads as if it had been painted on with a brush. In her nephew J.B.'s case, his brown hair was slowly drying and becoming a mass of curls – the curls being the bane of his existence as he was constantly teased about them at school.

"We have to tell the sheriff," Tillie began hesitantly after a few minutes of silence. "I'll have to go there . . . to his office. I hope he's not out somewhere in the county. Now, you three stay here. Stay here with Nellie.

I'll be as fast as I can, but it will take me a spell. You stay here! Understand? Don't leave Nellie by herself."

The three boys nodded their agreement, and after taking off the flowered apron that protected her blue and white checkered dress from grime when cooking or cleaning, Tillie quickly changed house slippers for anklets and oxfords and again reminded the boys to watch her daughter. Scurrying down the street and around a corner, she was soon out of sight. The three boys sat in silence. After all, there was not much left to say.

It was nearly an hour before Tillie and Sheriff Abel Taylor entered the kitchen. They had driven back to her home in his Ford sedan. The Wallton City Council and county commissioners had found the necessary funds to purchase three Ford automobiles for the small law enforcement department, one for Taylor and the others for the rest of the men. Still, the deputies' vehicles were used only in times of emergency in the county or at night by the deputy who patrolled both Main and Sixth Street, especially on the outer edge of Sixth where several bars had sprung up after the repeal of Prohibition. Occasionally, a brawl would erupt at one of the taverns, and the deputy would have to haul someone back to sit out a night in jail.

While Wallton and its surrounding area had a population of nearly 23,000, crimes involving serious injury or death were rare. Each of the company towns adjacent to the county's coal mines had their own law enforcement personnel to take care of any problems within their areas. Even in Wallton most crimes were of a minor nature, and the sheriff and six deputies usually patrolled on foot, doing ten-hour shifts, in or near the center of town.

"Now tell me what you told Mrs. Wellsby," Taylor said quietly," and don't all talk at once."

Both Anthony Wells and his little brother looked at John Bower who began hesitantly. "Well, we were all down in the creek . . . I know we shouldn't have been, but it was hot . . ."

"Fine," Taylor interrupted. "I don't care why you three were there. Just tell me what you think you found."

"We don't think," J.B. insisted. "We saw a body . . . a little girl. It was just lying at the edge of the bank in the weeds . . ." The other two nodded in agreement.

"You didn't touch the body, did you?"

"No, Sheriff, we didn't touch it. We didn't want to touch it!" Again the other two boys nodded in agreement.

Taylor looked at the boys for a minute, noting their disheveled appearance and the streaks of dirt on their faces left by perspiration. They were not lying. It was obvious that they had found something in the creek, and they were scared.

"Okay, I believe you saw something. I'm not sure what, but this is what I want you to do. You stay here with Mrs. Wellsby." He looked at Tillie who made no objection to his comment. "I'm going down to the creek and take a look. I don't want you three running around town and talking about a body until I know what's down there. I don't want the whole town upset until I know for sure what you saw. When I know, I'll come back, and you can go home. You understand me?"

All three boys answered, "Yes," and sat quietly as Tillie walked Taylor to the door.

It was the body of a small girl lying on her side in the shallow water and partly covered by a willow branch, one arm cradling her head. Taylor knew immediately who she was, the six-year-old child of Mary and David Gower, and knew he would have the dreaded job of telling her parents the sad news. Gently pushing the willow branch aside, he squatted near the body, careful not to get the seat of his trousers wet. For a moment, he could not see what had caused the child's death; however, as he gradually moved the white collar of her dress away from her tiny face, he could see bruises on her neck.

"Strangled," he muttered. "Looks like she was strangled. Now who could strangle a baby like this?" He shook his head in disbelief. He had seen dead bodies before, but a tiny dark curl floating lazily in the stream caught at his heart, and he inhaled deeply to stifle any sound that might emerge from his throat.

Taylor stood up and let go of the willow branch, nearly losing his balance in the sand and small rocks. He was a tall man, over six feet, with little body fat. A tan line occasionally peeked from under his hat as he spent most of his summer days out in the sun. He had donned fishing boots before entering the creek since he did not wish to get his regular shoes wet and felt it would be unseemly to go barefoot like the boys.

Carefully, he had rolled up the sleeves of his gray uniform shirt to keep the arms dry, but he could feel perspiration on his face and also felt the shirt sticking to his back. Taking a handkerchief from his pocket, he removed his hat and wiped the sweat from thick strands of brown hair and out of hazel eyes which were set far apart. Thirty years old, he still lived with his widowed mother and so far had not found anyone with whom he might contemplate marriage, not that there were many unmarried women over age seventeen in Wallton from which to choose.

As Taylor splashed through the shallow water and back up onto the opposite bank, he mulled over the sequence of actions he needed to take. First, he would go by the office of Dr. Fred Mason and get him to come and look at the body before he had it moved. The town was too small to employ a coroner, and Mason or Ted O'Connor, the town mortician, filled that slot whenever there was a death.

Then, after the doctor had made a cursory examination of the body, he'd go to O'Connor's Funeral Home and get O'Connor to remove the little girl from the creek. After that, he'd have to go and tell the parents. However, he decided to delay that chore until he knew for sure that the girl's father was home. That way if the mother became hysterical, as he assumed would be the case, he would have some help.

When Taylor reached the side of the bank where he had parked the Ford, he sat, pulled off his boots and put on his shoes. Fanning himself with his hat, he walked to the car and tossed his gear into the small trunk. It was nearing the middle of the afternoon, and he knew he had a number of stops to make and a return to the creek before he could release the three boys from Tillie Wellsby.

"What a way to spend a beautiful afternoon," he muttered to no one in particular, thinking of the trauma the boys had encountered. "Bet those three will think twice before they come back to the creek."

———————

"Doc, need to see you soon as possible," Taylor barked as he opened the door to the physician's examination room. The doctor and his elderly nurse, Norma, were completing a cast on the arm of a young man with jet black hair and eyes to match. Taylor didn't recognize the youth but thought he was probably about fourteen or fifteen years old. Although Norma had apparently tried to clean the boy up somewhat, Taylor could still see a light film of coal dust on his neck and around the edge of his hair.

Must be someone who got hurt at one of the coal mines Taylor thought. *Wonder why it wasn't taken care of out at the mine. Know there's a doctor paid by the mine owners who lives at one of the mines, takes care of those hurt in accidents, gives vaccinations, delivers babies. That doctor must have been busy at another mine.*

"Be with you in a minute," the doctor replied. He knew by the sound of Taylor's voice that something out of the ordinary had occurred. Putting the final touches on the cast, John Mason told his patient, "You've got to keep this in a sling. Can't use it for at least six to eight weeks."

When the boy began to protest that he needed to work, Mason cut him short. "I know. I know. You won't be getting any pay for all that time, but if that arm doesn't heal properly, you'll be off work a lot longer. So just quit your grumbling."

As his patient was ushered out, Mason beckoned for Taylor to follow him to his office, a tiny space next to the examination room with one grimy window that let in a bit of hazy light. Taking up most of the room was a battered oak desk cluttered with files, an overflowing ashtray, and an empty coffee cup. In front of it were two sturdy wooden chairs where patients sat as they told the physician their woes or occasionally received bad news.

A short man on a spare frame, Mason had a full head of light brown hair, gray eyes and a myriad of wrinkles on his forehead. Around the doctor's ears, Taylor noticed that the hair was showing a few strands of white. Mason's predecessor, Dr. Thomas Pearson, had retired and at age seventy-one could be called upon to help only in an emergency, like the smallpox epidemic a few years previously. Otherwise Mason handled all of the illness problems in Wallton, even making calls out in the county when people were too ill to come to town. He turned on a desk lamp, sat down heavily and peered at Taylor.

"Now, tell me what's so important that you got to rush in here and interrupt me when I'm with a patient?"

"Got a body, Doc. Down in the creek. A little girl."

"Drowned?" Mason interrupted.

"No, strangled, I think. That's why I want you to go with me right now before someone else sees her. Not enough water in the creek for her to have drowned unless she hit her head and fell. Doesn't look like that. I think she was killed, but I'd like to know what you think."

Immediately, Mason stood up, took off his shoes and the white coat he wore when seeing patients, and tugged a pair of scuffed boots over gray socks, a hole in one toe. Motioning Taylor toward the door, he grumbled, "Old Mrs. Welty's scheduled to be here in a few minutes. Gallbladder acting up again, I think. Let me get Norma to tell her that I may be away for a long spell. Welty won't like it, but that's how it will be."

The two men hurried to Taylor's auto, a battered three-year-old Ford Model A, and drove down Main toward the creek. Only a few people, mostly women doing a bit of shopping, were out on the hot sidewalks. Two of the stores, a J.C. Penney's and a corner drug store had front windows shaded by awnings, their dusty tan canvas limp and forlorn without any hint of a breeze. Near a tiny restaurant door, a grizzled dog huddled patiently, hoping that a bit of food might be tossed out.

"Going to go in over the bridge," Taylor explained as the car rattled across the span that connected the north and south parts of highway 85-87 which ran down the town's Main Street. "That way you can crawl down the bank where the body is, and I won't have to put my boots on again and wade across like I did earlier. Try to be careful as I want the vegetation disturbed as little as possible."

Mason nodded at the explanation and remained silent as Taylor parked the auto. The two men stood for a minute, looking down at the water. Then, holding on to a willow branch, the doctor began his descent into the creek. The drop was only a little over three feet in depth on the south side of the stream, but the bank was slippery with grass and weeds. Losing his balance, he slid down beside the body, his feet resting in the shallow water.

"Damn, didn't mean to do that but doubt that there was much on the side for me or you to see anyway. From the way the body is lying with the one leg partially underneath, she just may have been tossed down here."

"Tossed down? You don't think she was killed here?"

"No." If that was the case, you'd see where someone else probably would have slid down the bank . . . like I did. No, in my opinion she wasn't killed here. Nearby maybe, then carried from another place and dropped here. Must have been the case."

Mason shook his head and looked up at Taylor. "Why would such a little kid be down here at the creek by herself?" He rubbed his forehead thoughtfully and then said, "Don't think she was. Someone put her here.

Whoever did this probably thought no one would find her for several days. Maybe a coyote would have gotten to her before she was discovered." He stopped speaking, again bent over the body, and declared, "Strangled. Can see the bruises. No doubt about it. Wouldn't have taken much effort as she's so small."

"Nothing else obvious?" Taylor asked.

"No overt sign of molestation, if that's what you're asking, but O'Connor may have something else to say when he examines her more. Now, give me a hand."

Taylor grabbed Mason's hand and helped the doctor up the bank. Both men stood quietly for a few minutes, the silence broken only by the gurgling water and the horn of a passing car.

Finally Mason broke the silence. "Such a pretty child, all those curls . . . Well, better get O'Connor to take the body up to his funeral parlor soon. The water and this heat's doing some damage, and the flies are already on her."

For a few minutes Taylor stood outside O'Connor's Mortuary (usually referred to as the funeral parlor) and then slowly got in his car. Will O'Connor also had confirmed the strangulation and added that there were a few bruises on the girl's wrists which might have happened if she had struggled against her captor.

"Or could have happened when she was pulled forward or up toward someone's face. Doesn't weigh much so wouldn't have taken much to lift her up and grab her neck. Course, we'll never know for sure."

Taylor thanked O'Connor for his additional information, slight as it was, went outside and sat in his car. He began to mull over the incident, particularly the bruising.

Must have come up from behind her and grabbed her, and she might have got the bruises trying to get his hands loose from her neck. If she was pulled forward, she must have seen her killer . . . might have gotten bruised as she tried to pull away. Either way, it doesn't say who did it. As O'Connor said, may never know for sure . . . or the reason for it.

He shook his head and got ready to drive but hesitated and merely continued staring out the window. He had always considered Wallton to be a safe place to live, a place where residents knew their neighbors, a place where they helped each other in time of trouble, and a place where children could play without worrying about death lurking in bright sunshine on a hot summer day.

Of course, the town wasn't without some faults which involved him and his deputies. With jobs being so scarce, there was some minor theft and vandalism. Bar fights with injuries frequently erupted, and occasionally, very occasionally, someone was killed. A couple of ladies did provide special services to the town's single men. Still, they were not outright prostitutes, and as long as there were no complaints, Taylor and his deputies ignored the issue.

Taylor sighed and began thinking of what he had to do next. *Don't know what I can say to her parents but got to tell them. Wonder if the minister will be home by now. Certainly hope so. Don't want to face the mother alone. Also got to let those three boys go home soon from Tillie's; otherwise their parents will begin wondering why they ain't home for supper.*

Finally he started the engine and slowly drove the five blocks to the Gower's home which was located a block away from the town's First Methodist Church. The minister's car was parked at the side of the small brick house, one of the few in Wallton as most houses were constructed of wood or adobe.

The church congregation also had provided money for Gabriel Gower to have transportation as he frequently had to drive out into the county to comfort those too ill to come to church or to conduct funeral services. Many county residents, like Taylor and his mother, had small cemeteries where they buried their dead on their own land. Taylor hesitated as long as possible but knew he no longer could delay getting out of the auto.

"Welcome, Sheriff," the Reverend Gower greeted him from inside the screen as Taylor slowly walked toward the minister's open door. Gower was nearly as tall as Taylor, with a ruddy complexion and blue eyes behind thick glasses that made the eyes appear overly large. As usual, the minister was dressed in dark trousers and a white shirt but had already removed his coat and tie and rolled up his shirt sleeves.

"The missus is just getting ready to fry some chicken for dinner, and Annie always makes plenty, so you're welcome to come eat with us. I've just got to round up my brood . . . " Gower stopped talking when he saw Taylor's expression. "Not a social call?"

"No, Mr. Gower," Taylor began. "Could we talk a little further outside for a minute?"

"Certainly," Gower replied, coming out on his small porch and down three steps toward Taylor. "Dinner can wait if I'm needed."

There was no easy way to tell the man, Taylor knew. Informing someone that a relative was dead, particularly a member of the immediate family, was the most difficult part of Taylor's job. If it were a young person, the task could be even worse. As he tried to soften the blow, Gower stared at him in disbelief.

"Not my little girl!" he protested vehemently. "There's got to be some mistake. Not Jennifer."

Taylor merely nodded in the affirmative. "I'm afraid so. Down at the creek."

Still shaking his head, the reverend moved backwards, finally coming to sit on a porch step, his head in his hands. At about the same time a smiling Julia Gower appeared, her face flushed from cooking. Wiping her hands on her flowered apron, she came out the door and stood near Gower. Julia was much shorter than her husband with a round face, light brown hair, and what was known as a pug nose. Perspiration from cooking and the summer heat glistened on her nose and cheeks.

"You staying for supper, Sheriff?" Julia greeted Taylor. Then, noting the expression on Taylor's face and the position of her husband, she looked puzzled and asked, "What is it, Gabe? Bad news? Someone in the congregation hurt or did someone die?"

For a moment neither man responded. Turning to look at her, Gower quietly asked his wife, "Where's Jenny? Is she out back with the boys?"

"I'll go and see," his wife replied, as she smoothed the apron over her cotton dress. "I'll get the kids in the house now and get ready to go with you if you think you'll need me."

Julia started back toward the door when Gower stopped her and said in a pleading voice as he continued to look up at her, "Julia, please, please go see if Jenny is with the boys.

Noting the tears on her husband's face, she asked. "What? What? Is something wrong? Something with Jenny? Is Jenny hurt? Where is she? Gabe, where is she?"

When neither man responded, suddenly Julia Gower knew. "Oh God. O God! Oh my God! Dead? Not Jenny! Not my Jenny!" She began screaming and staggered toward the porch railing. "No, No, not Jenny!"

Both Taylor and Gower rushed to support her and get her back inside the home. Hearing the screams, Mrs. Davidson from the house next door came out onto her porch and called from across her yard, "Something wrong over there? Can I help"

Taylor knew it would only be a few minutes before the entire neighborhood would become aware of the tragedy as Mrs. Gower continued wailing. He also knew that he needed to get answers to some questions but realized that it would be impossible to talk with Julia Gower at that time. It had been all the two men could do to get the howling woman into the house and to a bedroom. As he stepped back outside, Taylor was confronted by Mrs. Davidson who by then had made her way from her yard to the Gower's porch.

"Something wrong, Sheriff? Anything I can do to help?" the woman again asked as she tried to peer through the screen door.

"Perhaps you can," Taylor replied calmly, blocking her view of the home's interior. After all, the reverend was hardly able to control his own grief, let alone that of his wife. Although the two didn't need prying eyes, the Gowers probably were friends with their neighbor, and her support might be welcome.

"Would you go see if you can round up the three Gower boys. I think they may be out back somewhere. Tell them to get in the house. Then maybe you could come and sit with Mrs. Gower for a spell. I'm going back inside as I need to talk some more with the reverend."

"Just let me take something off the stove," Mrs. Davidson replied as she scurried away and then arrived back at the Gower residence within minutes. She located the three boys out in the yard behind the house, herded them up to the residence, and went to sit with their mother. Taylor knew he would be unable to question Julia Gower at the present time, probably not until the next day at the earliest, as he could hear her still crying uncontrollably.

"Reverend, I know it's a bad time, but I've got to speak with your kids right now," Taylor explained after they left Julia Gower n the care of her neighbor. "I need to know if they were down at the creek with Jennifer. If not, I need to know when they last saw her. I realize this is a very, very difficult time for all of you, but I just have to try and find out how this horrible incident happened. Can you get the boys together, and perhaps we can go into another room for a few minutes."

"Let's go," Gower pointed to an open door but did not move. Although the man now was more composed, it was as if he could not think what to do. Finally, he rounded up his brood who were wide-eyed and silent.

"You can talk with them there, Sheriff, in the parlor."

The three boys clustered side by side on a gray upholstered sofa as their father slumped into a large wooden rocking chair. By now they knew that their sister was dead and could hear the continuing moans and sobs of grief from their mother. However, they didn't seem to know how they were expected to act, and all three kept their heads lowered, never meeting their father's or the sheriff's eyes. Taylor stood without saying anything for a few minutes, merely looking around the tiny room, its two window blinds drawn against the summer heat.

"When did you last see Jennifer?" Taylor asked quietly so as not to intimidate the boys. Immediately all three began talking, and their father had to shush them.

"Better talk to Mark first," Gower said. "He's the oldest. May make more sense. The younger two boys can fill in stuff if necessary."

Mark took a quick look at his father and then put his head down again. "We was just playing hide 'n seek," he stammered, "and, you know, Jennifer was 'it' and was hiding her eyes and counting. So we all ran down the alley and hid about a half a block away around the corner. We wanted to be sure it would take a while before she started looking and maybe found us."

"Did you see Jennifer leave the yard?" Taylor asked. "Did she follow you down the street?"

The boys looked at each other before Mark answered. "We never saw her after we left the yard."

"Didn't you think it was odd that she never came looking for you?"

"We must have just figured she'd given up looking for us." Mark glanced at his father and then back at Taylor.

"She never came," Matthew interjected. "So we just thought she wasn't going to play."

"Yeah," Mark responded. "We just went on down to Main and then came back home a little later."

"Didn't you wonder where your sister was?" Gower suddenly asked.

"No, I guess we didn't," Mark answered, still not making eye contact with his father. "We just thought she'd gone back in the house. You know, to get something to eat or to play with her dolls. Like girls do. We never thought anything bad would happen to her."

"But it did, didn't it?" Gower snapped and then shook his head. "Not your fault, boys. Nobody's fault." He sighed and looked at Taylor. "Can't watch them every minute. Can't keep them locked up, Sheriff. Kids got to play, and nothin' bad has ever happened to a kid before."

Not true, Taylor thought, recalling a similar incident in Wallton a few years previously. A young boy had been found dead, and that death was still unsolved, had eventually been ruled an accident.

"Ever see anyone strange around? You know, someone maybe just wandering through town? You boys are out and about like the rest of the town's kids. Haven't seen a stranger?"

The three boys shook their heads, and then the youngest, Luke, spoke up for the first time. "Well, there was that Gypsy. Remember guys? We all talked about the Gypsies 'cause of the funny way they dressed."

Taylor looked at the young boy. *Matthew, Mark and Luke. Wonder if the Gowers were hoping to name a kid John. Instead they got a Jennifer.*

"What Gypsy? When?"

"Down by the creek," Mark responded quickly. He didn't want Luke taking the answers to the questions away from him. "There were some Gypsies down there a few days ago. You know; they always come into town and camp there for a spell each summer cause there's water for their horses. Maybe Jenny ran into one of them if they came up town."

"How many times have I told you three not to wander down to the creek?" Gower interrupted harshly. "There's no one to see you down there. Anything can happen . . . You see what has happened to Jenny?" his voice faded into silence. What good would recriminations do? The damage had been done, and there didn't seem to be anyone to blame. The three boys could not be held responsible.

"It's getting late," Gower said quietly. "If we're done here, Sheriff, I need to see to my wife and try and get these hungry kids fed."

Taylor indicated that he had no more questions for the Gower boys at the present time, again extended his condolence to the reverend, and went out to his car. He knew that within the next thirty minutes, most of the town residents would have heard of the murder, probably from Mrs. Davidson as soon as she left the Gower residence. Immediately, the town's church women would begin cooking, and before the sun was up the next day, the Gower home would be filled with women bringing food and men attempting to comfort the father.

Taylor had offered to accompany Gower to the funeral home to make arrangements for the burial, but the reverend had indicated that he would go to make funeral arrangements with O'Connor later that evening or early the next morning. As he prepared to drive away, Taylor thought about the cost of the burial.

Wonder if they have enough money. Probably O'Connor will be kind enough not to charge for his service, but there's still going to be the cost of the coffin. Even for a child that probably won't be cheap. Wonder if the reverend has any savings. Can't imagine what it must be like, never knowing what your income will be . . . having to wait each Sunday after those attending the service are gone to see how much was put in the collection plate. What happens when not too many people show up? Money's tight now. People might not be able to give much. Course maybe those who know him will take up some kind of special collection to help out. I'll contribute, if I'm asked. Well, not my business I guess. Better get on home as I'm already late for supper.

So Taylor drove home, knowing that his mother already would have heard the bad news and preparing to answer the million questions she would ask.

Question him, she did. Where? When? Why? Who? Patiently, as he tried to eat the beef stew his mother had placed before him at their kitchen table, Taylor answered as best he could each question Nell Taylor asked.

His mother was not what people would call a fleshy woman for at five feet seven inches she was taller than most of her female friends and, even if she added a few pounds, always appeared to be slender. Her hair, which had once been a warm brown was now liberally sprinkled with gray, and she always wore it caught up with a comb on the back of her head. Never had Taylor seen her use makeup except for a dusting of rouge when she went to church or her Eastern Star meetings.

"Only bad women use makeup," Nell Taylor had explained when Taylor once questioned her. "That's also true of perfume," she added, her pale blue eyes sparkling. "A dab of lilac water is enough and is always in good taste."

Her family, the Watsons, had come to the area from Ohio several years after Wallton was already a small spot on the prairie. They had made a success of both ranching and farming as they had purchased land near a stream which usually produced enough water for a good stand of grass and a field of alfalfa that helped to feed the cattle and a few horses.

Levi Edson Taylor, Taylor's father, owned a large tract of land downstream from the Watson's place with a "sizeable" house and numerous outbuildings. He and his widowed father had been in the area over ten years when Nell Watson's family arrived, and he was known around the county as hardworking and honest when dealing with others. Over several years, Levi became a good friend to Nell's father, Paul Watson, and was frequently at the Watson home. Nell, the only female among four brothers, was considered to be pretty and "a catch" for some lucky man. At age seventeen Nell had married Levi Taylor, some fifteen years older than she, and one son was born to the union.

Ranching had been a good life for Levi and Nell, their son, Abel, and his grandfather, Lem Taylor. Abel became very fond of his grandfather, and the old man and the growing boy spent a great deal of time together wandering on horseback over both ranches. During his life the old man had traveled over a great part of the country and would recount numerous adventures.

Abel could remember a distant cousin who always called his grandfather Lemuel, and the old man would say quietly, "It's just Lem, Maude." Then later to his grandson he'd remark, "Ain't it funny Maude can't seem to bring herself to call me Lem. Seems like she don't feel it's a name." The name was short, it's true, as if in her haste to name him before she died, Lem's mother had found strength only for those few letters.

Abel knew his grandfather only when he was already an old man in his seventies. Unpretentious, Lem Watson usually wore gray cotton trousers and a gray cotton shirt, his trousers held up by ivory suspenders with a small red stripe in the center. High-top black shoes with knobby toes supported his ankles, and a gray felt hat, soiled from too much weather and handling, settled firmly over his fringe of white hair. Born a few years after the Civil War, Lem had lived for a time in Oklahoma when it was still called the Indian Territory. He had died one April just before Easter and was buried on a sunny spring day.

"Happy," they say, "is the bride the sun shines on." Happy, too, should be the mourners the sun shines on, for it would have seemed somehow easier for Abel to lay Lem away in sunshine.

A few years after his grandfather's death the original acreages were expanded, and both families continued to prosper. However, tragedy struck the Taylor family when Abel was fourteen. Levi Taylor was on the way home from Wallton with a load of grain when his horse was suddenly spooked by a coyote. The horse bolted, overturning the wagon. Levi was severely injured and died a few days after the accident.

With the help of neighbors and hired hands, Nell and Abel kept the ranch in good shape while Abel completed high school. Still, the boy could see that with his father's death and the hard ranch work, his mother's health was beginning to decline. Eventually he was able to persuade her to lease their property to a family living nearby.

"You don't have to sell dad's place," he had explained one evening late in May as the two sat quietly after the evening meal. "We will still own the ranch, but it's getting way too much for the two of us. I'll graduate soon, and I've got a pretty good chance to be hired as a deputy sheriff. We can get us a place in town, buy a house . . . or build one . . . wherever you want it. We will lease the ranch but still have some control over it. The lease money and my salary will provide us with a good income, and you know dad left quite a bit of money for both of us. In Wallton you'll be closer to some of your women friends and the church. You know how you always hate missing church during the winter months when we can't get into town because of the deep snow."

Eventually, Nell Taylor had concurred with his comments, and after several months of planning the two had moved into Wallton. Above the small business area at the upper end of the town, they had located a nice two-story house with a front room, dining room, fairly roomy kitchen and a screened back porch on the lower level. Up a curving staircase were three bedrooms and, to the delight of both, the luxury of an indoor bathroom. No longer would they have to trudge outside on cold winter night to get to the privy. Taylor took the front bedroom which had a door leading to a second-story porch so that he could exit the home without disturbing his mother if he were wanted for a night call. The extra bedroom became Mrs. Taylor's sewing room, and Taylor could usually find her there if he happened to come home in the middle of the day. His mother soon planted both a flower and vegetable garden and seemed content with her new living arrangements. Taylor certainly was.

After high school graduation, Taylor had been fortunate to get a job as a deputy with Sheriff Ralph Brown and settled into the routine of a Wallton law enforcement officer. Then, with over ten years as sheriff and considered an outstanding law enforcement officer, Brown died. None of the other deputies were interested in taking the job of sheriff, as there were extra demands on one's time, and no matter how hard one tried, it was impossible to please all of Wallton's citizens. Finally, Abel had been asked to "run" for the position in an upcoming election and won handily. He was not surprised at the election result, knew he had been elected as the only candidate running for that position, but vowed to himself that he would do his best to follow in Brown's footsteps.

Over twelve years I've been a deputy or the sheriff. Over twelve years! Doesn't seem that long. Where have all of those years gone? I'm getting old although I don't think of myself as old. Still . . .

"Those poor, poor people," his mother's words interrupted his thoughts. "What will happen to them now? How can they handle this?"

"They'll handle it the same way anyone would when there's a death," Taylor replied. "Granted, it's not an ordinary death . . . from illness or an accident. The little girl was killed, and I imagine they'll blame themselves for not watching her better. Still, you can't watch a kid every minute. You know that? You didn't always know where I was when I was growing up."

"I always thought I did, but now I know I didn't. Still, you were a boy. This is a little girl."

Taylor reached for another slice of his mother's home-made bread and the butter dish. She had just baked that day, and the bread was still slightly warm with the crust crisp the way he liked it. He wanted to mention that boys could get killed just as easily as girls; however, he didn't wish to get into a discussion on that issue.

"Mother, you might take some of this bread to the Gower family. I'm sure they'll get plenty of food, but none of it will be as good as your bread."

"I will. I will. First thing in the morning I'll bake fresh." He could see she was pleased by his comment. "I'll make a roast. Imagine they'll get a lot of cakes and pies, but it's meat and bread that sustain people in their time of grief. You'll drop it by for me?"

"Certainly. Just give the office a call when it's ready, and I'll be right over."

Will give me a reason to get out of the office for a few minutes he thought. *The place will really be jumping with people making up a reason to just drop by. A million questions. I'm sure we'll get a million questions. Won't be able to answer any of them, but that won't stop them from being asked.*

Taylor got up and carried his plate and glass over to the sink although his mother protested that she could clear the table. She always made the same comment about his helping her, just as she always hovered around the table, seldom sitting for over a few minutes and always jumping up to get him more coffee, add something to a dish, or sweep a few stray crumbs into her hand. He wondered if this was just a quirk of his mother, hovering over him, or if all women were trained to be immediately aware of what their men needed.

Moving into the living room, Taylor turned on the radio, an Atwater-Kent, which took a few minutes to warm up. Unlike many Wallton residents, he and his mother could afford this luxury.

Guess we're way above most folks. Have enough income for a comfortable house, a piano, a telephone. He moved the dial on the radio as sounds emerged. *Guess I'm not too late for the evening news. Might get a bit of Fibber McGee and Molly. If I'm lucky after that and there's no more trouble, I'll have a few minutes to myself to think about the murder and to get prepared for the onslaught of questions I'll get tomorrow.*

However, he couldn't concentrate on the news or the jokes spewing out of the radio from the comedy team. He could still see the lifeless body of the tiny Gower child and hear the wailing of her mother. Finally he decided to go for a walk, hoping the exercise would help erase the death scene from his mind and enable him to get some sleep.

By six o'clock the next morning, Taylor was in his office, drinking a cup of coffee from the thermos he had filled at home. All employees either brought food into work or ate at one of the few cafes in town. There were no facilities to prepare food in the building which consisted of a fairly large waiting room, a storage area, and Taylor's office. Located just off of the town's Main Street, it sat within a few feet from the town's small stone jail. It was Taylor's habit around 7:00 a.m. to stop by Willard's Café for a stack of pancakes or bacon and eggs. His mother complained that she could fix him "a nice breakfast," but he liked to be seen out and about early in the day as he felt it would show the public that law enforcement was always on the job.

Today, however, he knew that Willard's would be packed with other early risers, all of them with questions about who had killed the Gower child and asking what he was going to do about it. He sighed. He knew that he wasn't up to answering questions about the crime which so far had no answers. That also included any questions about the Gower family's reaction to the devastating news. The thermos of coffee would have to do for now; he'd think about more substantial food later in the day.

Just can't believe someone in this town would deliberately strangle a child. Can't understand what could have caused this. Not sure there'll ever be an answer to why the child was killed, but I'm gonna do my best to find the killer and learn the reason it happened.

He had read about murders being committed in larger cities, but he always had considered Wallton a very good place to live, a place where people did not have to fear harm, where they could be out day or night and be safe. The more Taylor thought about little Jennifer's death, the more questions came to his mind.

How did she get down to the creek without anyone seeing her go there? Couldn't have gone down one of the streets or someone would have seen her. Usually someone is outside even in the heat . . . or peering out a door or window. She must have been carried there. . . Did the boys lie to me? Did they hurt her and carry her down there? No, it would have been a struggle for them to carry her, and they'd probably have been seen. Must have been an adult. But who? If she didn't follow the boys, someone must have snatched her right out of the yard. But who? A gypsy? Who else would have been in the alley? Just too many questions, no answers.

A few minutes later one of the deputies, Arnold Drury, came in, leaving the door open so that the cool morning breeze would take any stale odor out of the place. "Morning, Sheriff," he said, the last word sounding like "shurf."

Drury was short and slender, his hair showing a few hints of white in its auburn color, and deep creases were visible underneath his brown eyes. He had been born in Wallton, worked for over ten years in the coal mines, been a deputy for nearly nineteen, and was married to a local woman whose appearance was very similar to his including auburn hair with patches of white. "Nothin' new, I guess."

"What could be new?" Taylor snapped and then was sorry that he had answered in such a brusque manner. "No nothing knew, Arn. No one has said they know anything, although it's only been a few hours since we found the body and the town-folk heard about it." He rubbed a shoulder which had begun to ache and wondered if he had pulled a muscle helping Mason and O'Connor get the Gower child's body out of the creek. "Just sitting here trying to figure out who could have done such a terrible thing."

"Maybe a transient?" Drury ventured, referring to the hordes of out-of-work men roaming across the entire country. "We still have quite a few wander through town every now and then even though we're sort of off the beaten path."

"Could be," Taylor stretched a bit and continued to rub the sore shoulder, grimacing slightly.

"Don't seem to see as many now as we did a couple years ago" Drury continued. "Seems like there may be a few more jobs around, particularly up north and with the C.C.C. in the mountains,"

Taylor grunted. He didn't particularly wish to be reminded of the Civilian Conservation Corps which had been established in 1933 by President Franklin Roosevelt. Two of his deputies had gone into the program, lived in work camps similar to military units, and provided national conservation work. They earned $30 per month like Wallton's deputies, and the sheriff could never understand why they had chosen what he considered would be a much more grueling job than the one they had abandoned.

"Don't get as many strangers as we had in thirty-two and thirty-three, Arn," Taylor agreed with the deputy and then asked. "Do you recall seeing anyone out of the ordinary yesterday?"

"No, but those guys know to go down the back streets. That's where they can usually get a handout from the lady of the house. Not much chance of food up here on Main."

Taylor knew this was true. Frequently his mother would mention that a transient had stopped by the house and that she had given the man a sandwich. He had cautioned her to be extremely careful, never to let someone unknown in the house, and to tell the men to look somewhere else for food. However, she ignored his advice as she felt sorry for those that were wandering the country due to the stalled economy and lack of jobs. She saved every scrap of meat left over from their meals and on Sunday evening would grind the scraps together, cut up some of her homemade dill pickles, add mayonnaise, and use the mixture to make sandwiches which she doled out to those who came asking.

"Well, wait until around nine, and then go knock on the doors of the houses near to the Gower home. Everyone should be up by then, and most will be eager to talk to you, even if they didn't see or hear anything. Be sure to ask if any of the women recall if a transient was in the neighborhood yesterday, someone asking for food or saying they'd do a chore for a meal and a place to sleep. Meanwhile, I'll take a run down by the creek. See if anyone is around there. Bound to be people down there soon, kids especially, to see what they can see. I'll ask them to move on. Don't want anything else happening, Arn, and we need to emphasize to people that they make sure their kids stay away from the creek for the rest of the summer."

"Sure thing," Drury replied as he got ready to leave. However, he knew that keeping people away from the creek would be almost impossible. The townsfolk would want to see where the crime occurred. that she had heard about the death. The deputy told her where he was going. Alma was hired to be

As Drury was leaving, Alma Lewis arrived, and the deputy told her where he was going. Hired to be the sheriff's secretary, Alma not only filled that role, she kept the place clean and also answered all phone calls, listening patiently to disgruntled people who called in complaining about noisy kids, dogs, and neighbors. Once someone called about a drop in water pressure as though the deputies could fix the problem.

A short, stout old maid who waddled when she walked, Alma was nearly sixty-three with brittle gray hair and an odor of being just slightly unwashed. Still no one commented about the body odor as she kept the place running smoothly, never responded to people's complaints with a harsh word, never gave out any information about arrests, and was loyal to both Taylor and his deputies. Taylor had often remarked that if anything happened to Alma, policing would come to a standstill in Wallton. His only problem with the woman was her tendency to hear and spread gossip about town. She would already know about Jennifer Gower.

"Going to walk up and see Doc Mason for a few minutes, Alma, but doubt he'll be able to add anything new," Taylor said as he took his hat and headed toward the door. "The other guys should be checking in soon. Know people will be stopping by, and calls are going to start coming in thick and fast. Just say we're working on the Gower case. Looking for anything. Asking for help. If anyone says they know something or saw something they thought was strange, be sure to take down their name and address or phone number if they're lucky enough to have a phone."

Alma nodded, placed a lunch sack on a nearby cabinet, deposited her purse in the middle drawer of her desk, and smoothed a wrinkle out of her navy cotton skirt as she sat down.

"Bet there won't be many kids out and about for quite a spell, Sheriff. Mothers will keep them inside or at least close to home."

"True, Alma. But you can't keep kids locked up, especially in the summer. They'll stay close to home today, but by tomorrow they'll be bored, looking for something to do . . . Can't keep bad things from happening. Just too bad it had to be the little Jennifer Gower."

Alma watched Taylor start up the street, and, as he had predicted, the phone began to ring.

———————◆◆◆———————

Arriving at the doctor's office, Taylor saw that there was a room full of people, and although they all looked inquiringly at him, he ignored their looks.

"Any chance he'll have a minute, Norma" he asked the receptionist who also did double duty as bookkeeper.

"Not likely, Sheriff. Already looks like a busy day. Something important come up? I could go tell him."

"No, nothing that can't wait. Just tell him I was here."

Taylor quickly backed out of the office before he could be asked about the murder. Not wishing to return to his office and face a barrage of questions, he decided to go on down to the creek. Parking where he and the doctor had been the previous afternoon, he stared at the water lazily making its way toward the east. He didn't really know why he was there or what he hoped to find, but he tugged on his boots and slid down the embankment near where Jennifer Gower's body had been.

Pushing aside weeds and small branches, he carefully scanned the place where the child had lain. Nothing. Only a small indentation in the side of the embankment, possibly caused by a portion of the body before it slipped further into the stream. Walking slowly up-stream several yards, he examined each side of the bank but could find nothing that indicated there had been any disturbance of any kind.

"Don't know what I'm expecting to see," he muttered. "Over night the water would have washed most anything away, if there was anything."

However, he decided to walk a little way downstream and under the bridge just in case something caught his eye although he wasn't looking for any particular thing. Then he discovered an empty Orange Crush bottle half buried in the mud, and he knew definitely that the three boys had not wandered that way. Soda bottles, particularly if they were not chipped, could be returned to a store for a rebate of a penny, sometimes two, and the boys would have grabbed it eagerly. He decided to pick up the bottle and eventually give it to Nell Welsby's nephew so that the boy could get some little money for the returned bottle.

As he slogged further through the water, careful not to stumble over the creek's rocky bottom, he noticed a tiny piece of paper lodged in a clump of grass, its bright yellow color not yet faded by the water. It was part of a candy wrapper, and he thought it might be from a small Butterfinger bar. Holding the bit of paper in his hand, he was puzzled by how new it looked and wondered how it had gotten in the creek and how long it had been there. Perhaps one of the three boys had discarded it as they waded through the water upstream, and it had floated down. People, kids especially, were not careful about what or where they dropped things. Then, as he stood looking at the bit of wrapper in his hand, he wondered if it might have belonged to Jennifer Gower, have slipped from her hand, and have floated away from her body.

Just the thing to entice a little girl. A piece of candy. All kids like candy. If what I'm thinking is true, then her killer didn't have to carry her down to the creek. She went with him for the candy. Money's scare, and a kid will do most anything for some candy, and she must not have been afraid of him.

He shook his head sadly. Slowly, it began to dawn on him that Jennifer had not been afraid, might even have recognized her killer, possibly had seen him about town or at church. Just another resident of the town.

"She would have gone up to him willingly for the candy," Taylor exclaimed aloud. "She would have. She wasn't afraid of him. She knew him. Shit! She knew him!"

Funeral services for Jennifer Gower filled the church and the vestibule with people standing along the side and back walls. The small pine coffin looked as forlorn as a scraggly mum in late November. It sat in front of the pulpit's oak railing, a tiny spray of multi-colored roses on top. A minister from a town to the north had been called to do the eulogy, and the Methodist choir which consisted of nine people sang traditional songs – *Nearer My God to Thee* and *Amazing Grace.*

After the congregation recited the *Lord's Prayer*, the coffin was taken from the church by six pallbearers, although one mourner remarked that it was so small only four were needed. Jennifer Gower was to be buried two blocks away at the Protestant cemetery on the northwest side of town which was customary. Catholics always were buried in St. Catherine's Cemetery located up a small hill at the southern end of Wallton.

Taylor followed toward the back of the procession, his eyes carefully scanning the mourners. With only a few exceptions, Taylor being one of them as he was in uniform, the men were dressed in suits or various types of jackets and trousers. Both City Councilman Cecil Keller and George Allen, President and owner of Wallton's First National Bank, were in hats, light-weight summer suits and ties of subdued color. Most of the men appeared to be extremely uncomfortable in the July heat, and some wiped sweat from off their foreheads. When they neared the tiny scar in the earth where the coffin was to be placed, all of the men removed their caps or hats.

Is Jennifer's killer here? Taylor wondered, trying not to be obvious as he carefully watched the mourners. *No, why would he come? On the other hand, why wouldn't he? If the child knew him, the family probably did. Would look odd if he weren't here, especially if he were a member of the church. Someone would notice his absence. He would need a very good excuse not to be here. Even those lucky enough to be employed have taken a few hours off from their jobs, especially members of Gower's congregation.*

As the minister began speaking, Taylor drew nearer to the crowd, noting that most of the women were clustered together and dressed in some form of traditional black. Many wore short sleeves with patterns of small dots or various types of flowers on a sheer or silky dark background. A few of their garments were obviously more suited for autumn as they had longer sleeves and seemed to be of a sturdier material. *Probably can't afford a new summer dress but know black is the traditional color for funerals. Must be sweltering in this sun.*

All of the women wore white gloves, and Taylor wondered if this were a mark of summer fashion or because the women's hands were probably red and rough from numerous household chores. Most of the women mourners carried small paper fans, and their constant movement back and forth in the air made Taylor think of insects fluttering around the female faces.

Taylor idly noted that the Gower boys were not in attendance. This was not unusual, however, as until children were in their teens, they usually were protected from the trauma of birth and death.

Perhaps, he thought, *another reason the boys are not at the funeral service is because Reverened Gower would realize that townspeople might think the three should have protected their little sister. Funny how people always need to blame someone even if that person is faultless.*

Julia Gower, supported by her husband and another man, her brother from Kansas Taylor had been told, continued to sob uncontrollably. As the minister concluded with "ashes to ashes, dust to dust," she sank to the ground and was carried from the group by several mourners. Quickly the congregation began to disperse and return to the church basement for the usual quantities of food always served after a funeral. However, Reverend Gower remained at the gravesite, and Taylor also remained, standing silently to one side as the reverend knelt and prayed. When the tiny coffin was finally covered with earth by the workman from the funeral home, Gower placed five roses on top of the fresh soil. *One from each surviving member of the family,* Taylor wondered but didn't ask.

"Why?" Gower gasped as he struggled to rise from the grave. "Why? . . . Why? I can't understand. Who would kill a child? Just a tiny girl, Sheriff. Who could do such a thing?"

Taylor had no answer and said as much. He had no idea who the individual was but had begun to think, actually felt certain, that it was someone both he and the minister knew or at least had encountered. However, he did not say this to Gower as he gently placed a hand on the grieving man's shoulder.

"I don't know, Reverend. My men are out scouring the town, hoping someone saw something. Come! Let me walk back with you to the church. A lot of your friends are there, and Mrs. Gower will need your support."

The reverend nodded his agreement, and the two men silently made their way from the gravesite to the church. The large basement, its linoleum floor mopped spotless, felt unusually cool in the noonday heat. It was filled with people quietly talking and eating the wide variety of food prepared by the females of the congregation. Taylor noted that his mother, a white apron over her black dress, was busy replenishing platters of food. Julia Gower sat in one corner with two women, each holding one of her hands. Gower immediately went to his wife's side and knelt before her, talking quietly and wiping tears from her face.

Taking a plate, Taylor helped himself to a bit of meat casserole and green beans and moved to a corner. He was not particularly hungry but felt taking food was expected of him. Within a few minutes he was surrounded by men asking if he had any information about the killer. Some suggested that it was a stranger passing quickly through town without being noticed; several others indicated that it must have been "some insane person;" only one mentioned that the killer might still be in Wallton. Although Taylor was surprised by the comment that the killer might still be among them, he merely took in all of the suppositions and suggestions and kept repeating that his men were out trying to find someone or some little thing that would point to the culprit.

Eventually, George Allen caught Taylor's attention and motioned him over.

"Drop by the bank tomorrow or the next day, Sheriff, if you can find a minute" he said as Taylor made his way to the man's side. "Maybe I can do something that will help you find the killer."

Although he had no idea what Allen could do, Taylor was not about to offend the man. Allen's family had been among the first settlers of Wallton and was both prominent and wealthy. They owned a great deal of ranch land west of Wallton and were also involved in mining and lumber. One of the Allens had been mayor of Wallton years before, and another had been elected to the state's House of Representatives. While Taylor's own family was somewhat prosperous and well-known, especially among the farming and ranching community around Wallton, he had learned from what his mother occasionally said that they were not in the same social class as the banker's family. "A bit above us" was the way his mother put it.

"Certainly will." Taylor replied as another man waiting to talk with the banker tugged at the man's sleeve. "If not tomorrow, Mr. Allen, next day for sure."

Late that evening Taylor waited in his car outside Doc Mason's home. He realized that he knew very little about the doctor and had occasionally wondered why the man had settled in Wallton. He would never ask as he knew that would be an invasion of privacy and probably resented by the physician. Maybe old Doctor Pearson had enticed Mason to take over his practice when he eventually retired.

It was a typical Wallton summer night, hot but with a slight breeze that carried the scent of marigolds from a yard down the street. Mason's home was a small white house with green shutters and was situated at the back of a large yard which made the house look even smaller. Taylor knew from local gossip that the man' wife, considerably younger than her husband, had died several years previously. Mason had never remarried but still kept the home in pristine shape.

"Mabel would look down and yell at me if I didn't keep the place up," Mason once had joked to Taylor.

From across the street and through an open screen door came the sound of someone practicing scales on a piano. *Nice night* Taylor thought as he watched twilight edge across the sky and turn it from pale pink and orange to a deep purple A cluster of gray clouds hovered toward the south, an indication that there might be a bit of rain later in the night. A slight breeze rattled the leaves of two large cottonwood trees in the doctor's yard. Shortly, Taylor heard the sound of Mason's car and got out as the doctor pulled up behind him.

"Not more trouble, I hope," Mason exclaimed as the two met. "I'm dog tired."

"No, just wanted to talk over something private. You're the only one I can talk seriously with and not have it blabbed all over town, but it can wait." Taylor could see that just lugging his medical kit was putting a strain on the older man.

"Didn't mean to put you off." Mason protested, pleased at the compliment about his keeping information private. "Come on in. You had supper? I can find something for us to eat."

"Yep. Had my ten-course meal that my mother always prepares," Taylor replied laughing, "but if you're sure, I'll keep you company for a few minutes."

The two men made their way into Mason's home, and Taylor sat at the kitchen table covered with flowered oilcloth and waited while the doctor prepared a scrambled egg, sliced a large tomato, and buttered a slice of bread. Compared to the meal Taylor usually had in the evening, it looked extremely frugal. However, the doctor appeared to think it was adequate and, after eating and taking the dishes to the kitchen sink, suggested the two men sit in his back yard. "Cooler out there," he said as he held the screen door.

Taylor was amazed at the yard. While the front of Mason's home had a small bit of lawn, something lacking from most homes in Wallton, the back yard was a blaze of color. Dahlias, some of their blossoms almost as large as dinner plates, were staked in rows at one side. Lavender, pink, and white stalks of larkspur swayed in an occasional bit of breeze. Interspersed with clumps of nasturtiums were asters, heavy with buds. Morning glory vines covered a fence on one side, their blossoms curled and waiting for the morning sun, while rows of hollyhocks towered against the opposite fence.

At the rear of the lot was a small shed, for various tools Taylor supposed, and around it were the usual bunches of Bouncing Betty weeds.

"Helps me relax after a busy day of Mrs. Welty's gallbladder problems," Mason explained as he waved a hand toward the flowers and lit a cigar. He didn't offer Taylor one as he knew the man didn't smoke. "Nothing like getting your hands in dirt. Must be a holdover from childhood."

"Amazing," Taylor said and added, "Just beautiful. My mother would be envious."

Taylor could tell that Mason was pleased by his comments, and the two men sat quietly for a few minutes, just enjoying the silence. Finally Mason asked, "Why the visit? Not just to look at the flowers, right?"

"Well, I always enjoy your company of course, and you're about the only person in the whole town I trust to talk to right now." Taylor hesitated for a moment and then continued. "This afternoon I took a walk back down in the creek and found something that bothers me," Again Taylor hesitated for a bit as if gathering his thoughts. "I want you to hear me out . . . see if you think I'm crazy or making too much of it. Might be something or might be nothing, but it's been bothering me all the rest of the day."

"Well, just spit it out," the doctor exclaimed. No use hemming and hawing about."

"I think the Gower girl knew her killer."

"What?" Mason sputtered. "Knew her killer?"

Taylor took his time explaining about his return to the creek and discovering the empty soda bottle. He particularly emphasized the candy wrapper.

"Well, your thinking's okay about the soda bottle," Mason agreed after a few moments of silence. "If those three boys had gone under the bridge and further down the stream, they immediately would have grabbed the bottle and have been overjoyed to have found it. However, that candy wrapper could have been lodged in the grass for several days or even longer as you know the creek's water is particularly low at this time of year. It wouldn't necessarily have been discarded by the dead girl. Could have been there for days, maybe even weeks just waiting for the water to rise high enough to wash it away."

"I guess you're right." Taylor had listened and carefully considered Mason's comments, eventually nodding in agreement. "Might even have washed down from way up stream near those picnic grounds in the hills. Probably has nothing at all to do with the Gower girl's death. Also, someone might have been walking into town and just tossed the wrapper off the bridge. Probably that's what happened 'cause the paper was not particularly faded."

"Now, just hold your horses," Mason protested. "I'm not saying it didn't belong to the little girl. Most likely it did. However, I'm just trying to look at all of the possibilities, as I'm certain you have. And, I hate to say it, but I think you may be right. Now that I look at it, I think Jennifer Gower at least had seen her killer about town. She probably wasn't particularly afraid of him, went with him willingly. Doubt if you're gonna tell her folks that."

"No," Taylor replied emphatically. "It's bad enough that they think a stranger did it, and maybe it was a stranger. Maybe I'm barking up the wrong tree. Still you and I are aware of this other possibility, the only ones aware of it. The only ones! Haven't even mentioned it to my deputies or anyone else. Won't mention it. If word got out that I thought the killer might be a local person, we'd have the whole town looking over their shoulders at each other, accusing anyone they didn't like for whatever reason."

Mason knew what Taylor was saying and agreed. "Don't need any additional problems. Only you and I are thinking it might be someone local. Won't mention it to a soul," he emphasized nodding his head, and added, "Sure hope we're wrong though."

"Well, thanks for listening to me, crazy as my idea seems. I just had to talk it over with someone, someone who could see the possibility. Don't have too many people that I can trust to just listen and not talk. I'll say goodnight now as it's getting late, and it's been a long day. Know you're tired. I know I am."

Taylor got up, stretched and started around the corner of Mason's home. Pausing for an instant he said, "By the way, I've got to go to the bank and see Mr. Allen sometime tomorrow. Don't know what it might be about; Allen asked me to drop by. That's the way he put it – 'drop by'."

———◆———

The next morning Taylor made his way to the First National Bank, the most imposing building in Wallton. Constructed of two floors of red brick with doors and windows delineated by sandstone blocks, it dominated a western corner of Main Street. Taylor climbed the heavily polished stairs to the second floor and waited as a local farmer whom Taylor recognized as living out east of town nodded to him and started down the stairs. Sitting at a neatly ordered desk was Allen's receptionist and secretary, a thin woman with wispy blonde hair pulled back in a bun. She smiled at Taylor and said, "He shouldn't be too long now, Sheriff."

"That's all right, Barbara. I've got a few minutes to spare. That a new dress you're wearing? Very pretty color."

Barbara Hershey blushed and smoothed the lace collar of her dress. "Well, yes, it is, Sheriff. Nice of you to ask. It was on sale at Penney's, and I've always been partial to anything blue." She smiled at him again and turned back to her typewriter.

Must have said the right thing. Doubt if she gets too many compliments, although maybe she does. I don't really know anything about her other than the fact that she's single. She must not want to marry for if she did, there are a lot of single men around the county. Would help her looks if she did something with her hair, soften her face a bit. Don't think I've ever seen her with a man, but that doesn't mean anything. I'll ask my mother; she's bound to know if there's anything to know. He shook his head. *No, better not ask mother. She'll immediately think I'm interested in Barbary Hershey, mention my asking to some of her friends, and that'll start tongues wagging all over town.*

"Come on in, Sheriff," George Allen said as he shook Taylor's hand and ushered the man into his office. Allen was a large man, slightly shorter than Taylor, with graying hair and pale blue eyes made larger with glasses. Although it would be another stifling summer day, the banker was dressed in a three-piece suit of gray gabardine, a stiff-collared white shirt, and a conservative navy tie with small white scrolls. "Didn't mean to keep you waiting as I know you've got a lot on your mind and a lot to do."

"Well, I've got a lot on my mind. That's for sure. But I don't seem to have much to do as we haven't come up with anything new. Just have no idea who killed the little Gower child."

Taylor took the seat offered him, noting the massive oak desk and two matching bookcases next to a large window which provided a view of the north side of Wallton. A small fan was attempting to stir the air, and Taylor glanced at the desk set which held ink and two pens, noting that it had an onyx base. On a wall over the banker's desk was a painting of an older man with a full beard. *Must be his* father, Taylor thought and was very aware when Allen settled into the swivel chair at his desk that the banker made certain his head was turned half away from the sheriff.

Poor guy. Must be hell living with that handicap. Certainly glad it's not me. Don't know if I could handle it like he does.

George Allen's handicap was a badly disfigured left side of his face which he always kept turned away from people when talking to them. Like everyone else in Wallton, Taylor knew the story behind this action. Allen had been born with his left eye several inches below his right eye and an ear that was considerably smaller than his other ear and faced backwards from his mouth. When he was younger, the left side of his mouth drooped almost to the bottom of his chin; however, that did not seem to affect his speech, and extensive surgeries at an out-of-state hospital had corrected the drooping mouth problem to a great extent but did nothing for the rest of his face.

Allen had been the brunt of much teasing as he entered school, with children calling him a monster or a freak. To avoid the taunts, he had spent most of his childhood after the fifth grade with a tutor, with his parents, and with an older sister, Gwendolyn. He had never married and now at age fifty-four, according to town gossip, probably never would. Although he was well-known and respected in Wallton and throughout the state and was said to have a small circle of friends, most people who needed to do business with Allen shied away from looking at or talking directly to him. Taylor made certain that he was looking directly at the man.

"Maybe I can help you out a bit," Allen began. "Sometimes people know more than they think they do. Maybe they saw something; maybe they heard an odd noise of some kind. I'd be willing . . . well, actually the bank would be willing to put up a reward. Say five hundred dollars for any worthwhile information."

Five hundred dollars! For a minute Taylor couldn't respond. Five hundred dollars was a great deal of money, especially when most families who had men lucky enough to be employed only had income of about thirty dollars a month. Even as sheriff, Taylor's salary was only seven hundred dollars a year, and for that amount he was expected to be available seven days a week. Nights, if needed. "That's over a year's pay for most families," he blurted out.

"Yes, I think it is," Allen responded quietly. "However, it would be worth the money if we could learn something."

"True, but it would have to be something worthwhile. That kind of money will bring all sorts of information, most of it worthless. You'd need to say that the reward would only be paid if it led to us finding the killer."

"And getting a conviction," Allen added as he straightened several papers lying on his desk. "I'd want the man put away for a good long spell, maybe executed." He stopped speaking for a minute and then continued.

"I guess it was a man, right? Can't imagine a woman killing that little girl, almost a baby."

"Pretty sure it was a man," Taylor said, "but you've brought up a point." He had not considered that the killer might be female, not until Allen made his last comment. He thought back to what he and Doc Mason had discussed the previous night.

Perhaps the Gower child would have been more willing to go with a woman, more like her mother . . . less scared of a woman. The kids who found the body had mentioned the Gypsies, but why would a Gypsy woman kill a child? No! I feel that the killer was male.

"This is what . . . the second or maybe the third kid that's died over the past several years from something other than a disease?" Allen asked. "I'm pretty certain that it's been several."

"Three as I think I recall hearing about, Mr. Allen. A young boy when I was just a deputy. Then another boy a couple of years later, up by the rail yard. However, he wasn't strangled. It looked like he'd been hit in the head with a large chunk of coal, and since he was found right close to the rails, it was thought he'd been too near the moving train, and a chunk of coal fell off and hit him. Certainly could have done that."

"I do remember that's what people thought at the time," Allen responded and then after a minute asked. "You feel that way?"

"Well the other boy that was found up by the rails a year or so later . . . twenty-five or twenty-six I think it was . . . sometime around there . . . appeared to have been strangled, just like the little Gower girl. So that must have been a killing not an accident. Maybe the other one was, too." Taylor paused and then added, "We've told the kids to stay away from the tracks, but both the trains and the creek just seem to draw them, 'specially the boys. First time it's been a girl."

Both men sat silently for a few minutes, each thinking back over the previous deaths. Then Taylor abruptly stood and said, "Well, I'll not take any more time out of your busy day. Certainly do appreciate you coming forward with the reward. You gonna go to the newspaper office? Talk with Dawson? Ought to be something in the paper about it."

Taylor was referring to Mel Dawson and the *Wallton Weekly* to which almost every household in Wallton subscribed. Since, only a few people had radios, the *Wallton Weekly* was their lifeline for both the news of the world and their local news, particularly recent deaths and mention of anyone from out of town visiting relatives.

"Yes, I'll make certain to let Mel know," Allen replied as he stood and walked Taylor toward his office door. "Paper won't be out for a couple more days, but as soon as I call Dawson, the news will get out anyway. Most people know the news before the paper is printed." He chuckled and then added, "Please let me know, Sheriff, if there is anything else I can do to help you and your officers."

Taylor shook Allen's hand, said a quick "goodbye" to Barbara Hershey, who blushed again, and made his way through the bank's lobby, nodding at several people as he left.

———◆◆◆———

Instead of returning immediately to the office, Taylor decided to drive home and grab a bite of lunch. He seldom went home except for dinner but knew that his mother would have something with which he could make a sandwich – or she could make one for him – and then quickly get back to his office. However, this time he was wrong.

The entire Taylor living room was filled with a quilting rack with several women surrounding it. Busy hands were taking tiny stitches in various pieces of brightly flowered cloth as the women attached images of flowers and leaves to a white background of muslin stretched across the rack. Taylor stood quietly surveying the scene while words and laughter surrounded him.

Finally one of the women, a Mrs. Sanford he thought, noticed him and said, "Sheriff! Heavens, we're so noisy we didn't hear you come in."

"What's wrong?" Nell Taylor asked, immediately rising from her chair and making her way around the edge of the room.

"Nothing. Nothing's wrong, Mother," Taylor answered. The women had all stopped talking and were peering at him anxiously. "I just decided to come by to get a bite to eat. I can make myself a sandwich. You just sit back down and go on doing what you were doing."

However, his mother continued toward the kitchen, and Taylor was deluged with questions from the group before he could follow her. "Anything new? No idea who did it? How are you going to find the guilty person? Have you seen the reverend recently? You'll find the person, won't you?" Taylor merely answered "yes" or "no" as he edged out of the room, and by the time he entered the kitchen, his mother had donned an apron and had a plate of food on the table.

"Sorry, mother. I guess I didn't think about you having company."

"Just the usual ladies. We're making a quilt for the Gowers. Thought it might help ease their grief to know my church circle is thinking of them. I'll leave you to your lunch."

Taylor nodded. He hadn't realized that his mother had a church circle. In fact, he wasn't certain that he knew the meaning "church circle." Was it connected to the church, or was it merely a group of women who went to the same church and met regularly? He seemed to realize that sewing the quilt pieces together probably would take several meetings over several weeks and assumed the meetings would all be held in the Taylor front room so that the quilting apparatus would not have to be taken down and then reassembled.

I guess I never thought much about my mother, about what she does on a daily basis. Other than take care of me, what does she do? We're both up early every morning, and she's usually eating her breakfast as I go out the door. Then what is her day like? Cleaning? Laundry? Going to the grocers? Preparing our supper? I know she goes to church regularly and to a monthly Eastern Star gathering, and now I know she has a sewing circle.

Taylor shook his head as he got up and took his plate to the sink. Carefully he washed it and set it aside to dry on a towel. From the living room came the chatter of the women and an occasional laugh. He wanted to go out the back door and avoid the group but knew his mother would be unhappy if he did so.

"Well, ladies, I'll leave you to your work and get back to mine," Taylor smiled as he inched his way around them. "I may be a little late tonight, mother, but not too late."

He quickly made his exit and got in his car but didn't drive away, just sat idly staring out the window. *It's true. I don't really know my mother. Oh, I know who she is as my mother, but I don't know much about her or my dad for that matter. I guess they loved each other. Guess I'll have to assume they did although they hardly ever showed any affection toward each other.*

I hardly remember my dad and even then only as a young boy. I missed him when he was killed, and I'm sure my mother did also. I remember her crying at the funeral, but she didn't cry at home . . . at least not when I was around or awake. I'm sure it was a terrible loss to her . . . or I guess it was. Still, she just went on as usual as most folks have to do . . . as the reverend's family will have to do.

He started the auto and slowly moved down the quiet street, noticing a shaggy stray dog nosing around outside a corner home. Rubbing the side of his head, he continued thinking about his family.

I wonder if kids ever know their parents or if parents ever really know their children. Does anyone ever know anyone else . . . really know what that person is, what they want, what they think or believe, what they fear . . . what they might be capable of doing . . . Well, I guess there's only thing I know for sure. Whoever killed Jennifer Gower has to be found.

During the next few weeks, even though he felt after his last talk with Dr. Mason that it would be of little use, Taylor followed what the town's residents, and his mother's church circle, would expect as police procedure. The citizens wanted to know that Wallton's police were working on the murder, wanted to know that people were being questioned, wanted a killer apprehended. Taylor had his deputies again go house-to-house seeking to glean any bit of information that might lead to a murderer. It was a total waste of time. No one recalled seeing anything that could be called out of the ordinary or no person unknown to the area residents.

Thinking that the three boys who had discovered the Gower girl's body might have overlooked some minor detail when talking with him the day of her death, Taylor spoke with them again, individually and as a group. He gave them the empty soda pop bottle he had found in the creek and asked if it had belonged to one of them. All said the bottle was not theirs although they were glad to get it and eager to reclaim any money due from its return to its original seller.

Apparently, they had not gone to the creek down Main Street. "So that no one would see us going to the creek and tell on us" was their explanation. The only person the boys mentioned who might have noticed them about two blocks from the creek was "old Mrs. Schooley out sweeping her front porch. We just ran by as quick as possible," John Bower explained. "We knew she'd scold us and tell us not to go down there."

To verify this explanation, Taylor called on Mrs. Schooley, a plump white-haired widow whose husband had been dead for nearly ten years. If it were approved by the elected officials, she'd soon be a recipient of the state's old-age pension granted to anyone who was sixty-five years of age and had been a resident of the state for five years.

"Saw the three boys," she said, nodding her head as the two stood on her tiny front porch, its surface gleaming from a recent coat of varnish. "Didn't see no stranger, just them boys, and they was sure in a rush. They weren't lookin' to talk with me."

Brushing a stray strand of white hair away from her eyes, she smoothed the apron spanning her ample hips. "Knew they were on their way to the water, but didn't call out to them. It weren't any of my business though. Not my business to keep track of other people's kids. Kids always want to play in the water. Seems like you can't keep them away. I remember I liked it when I was a little girl."

Taylor nodded in agreement, thanked the woman for her comments, and knew he would have to look further for a possible witness. As residents from around the county came into town, usually to purchase a few groceries or farm supplies, they also were questioned, particularly about strangers. None remembered noticing anyone unknown on the county roads or anyone walking or camping in their fields or pastures. To most of the town's residents it seemed some individual had just mysteriously appeared, strangled Jennifer Gower, and then mysteriously disappeared.

Recalling the young man he had seen in Doc Mason's office the afternoon of the discovery of Jennifer's body, Taylor wondered if his injury might have occurred if he had been the individual who killed the little girl. Although he felt it was extremely unlikely, he considered that Jennifer might have been lured near the man, a boy really, and her struggle to free herself from his grasp had caused the injury. Perhaps the man had lost his footing while descending the river bank carrying the child and had broken his wrist as he tried to stop his slide into the water. Taylor felt that also was unlikely and that the killer was a Wallton resident, but to check out any possibility, he decided to drive the seven miles out to that coal mine and see if the young man with the broken arm was still there.

The company town run by the coal mine owners was a barren sight as, unlike Wallton, there was almost no vegetation surrounding it. Situated in a draw off a narrow dirt road, the ruts caused his Ford to bounce up and down. Because of the summer heat, Taylor had to drive with windows down, and a thin film of dust blew into the car and settled in the sweat on his face. *Probably look like something the cat dragged in* he mused as he mopped his chin with a damp handkerchief already showing grimy traces of brown.

Finally locating the mine superintendent's office, he noted several scraggly trees in front, all looking like they would not survive the rest of the summer. Away from the office tiny identical wooden houses, shacks actually, were sprinkled across the hillside, each near a privy, and occupied by those miners who had families, Taylor could see two small dogs and numerous children scattered in the unfenced yards as they chased a ball or played what he thought might be a game to tag. Two large structures badly in need of paint housed any unmarried men, while what appeared to be a relatively new company store and bar completed the dreary scene. A steady breeze tossed dust and bits of sand high into the summer sky.

Checking with the superintendent, Taylor was directed to the mine foreman and learned that the young man in question was in his family's residence with his arm still encased in the cast. The break, he was told, had been caused in a minor accident while a coal car was being unloaded and had tipped over. With this confirmation, the list of Taylor's possible suspects, although there was never actually a list, dwindled to zero.

Nearly four months had passed since the funeral for the little Gower tot. Children were back in school from 8 a.m. to three-thirty in the afternoon, and autumn was in full swing. In the hills surrounding Wallton the aspen had already dropped golden leaves, their white bark stark against the surrounding dark green pines and cedars. Early morning temperatures hovered in the low forties, and people welcomed the sun, no longer complaining if sixty degrees occasionally was reached by late afternoon. Tops of the mountains had been dusted with snow for several weeks, and some of the old-timers predicted a harsh winter.

So far, the huge reward offered by banker Allen had turned up no reliable information regarding the murder of little Jennifer Gower. At first, there had been numerous telephone calls, along with Wallton residents stopping by the sheriff's office to report someone they thought might have been a "bit suspicious." When these few "suspicious" individuals were dutifully investigated, all had plausible reasons why they could not have been the murderer. Most were indignant about being questioned and voiced their displeasure loudly.

With nothing helpful from Wallton's population, Taylor and one of his deputies began seeking information from individuals of coal-company towns located even further from Wallton. All the individuals questioned could show that they had been at work, most deep underground. As Taylor learned, few of the mine workers had access to automobiles, and many had not even learned to drive after immigrating to America. Covering the ten or more miles into town would have required a time-consuming walk for an individual and probably would have been noticed by anyone driving to or from Wallton.

In addition, since the company towns were located quite a distance off the main highway and, with the exception of the superintendent, were populated by families or individuals whose pay envelopes scarcely covered necessities, wandering hobos were seldom seen in their vicinity seeking food or money. Handouts there usually were scanty. No one recalled seeing any wanderers around the time of the Gower girl's death.

During the first four or five weeks after Jennifer's burial, Reverend Gower would come by the office every two or three days to see if any new information had dribbled in.

"Nothin' new, Sheriff?" he would inquire, dropping heavily into a chair in front of Taylor's desk.

"Nothing, Mr. Gower, but I want to assure you that all of us, both me and my deputies, are still working on it. We're sure to find something."

However, the reverend soon gave up these visits when Taylor had to keep telling him that no worthwhile information had come forward. Courteously, Taylor always walked the minister out of his office and to the building's door and watched as the man started up the street, his head down and his steps slow.

Must be terribly painful for him getting up every morning and knowing she's gone, Taylor thought. *Not knowing why it was done or who did it. Wonder how his wife is? Hope she's much better than the few times I've seen her when I went to their home. Mom said she hasn't seen Mrs. Gower or the boys at the church since the funeral. Don't know what we can do for that family. Know the reverend wants to learn who killed his little girl and why, but while I think it may be someone local, we just haven't been able to come up with any suspect. Seems like the killer just vanished into thin air.*

———◆———

"Bit chilly for October," Deputy Salvatore Musso said as he entered Taylor's office. Of Italian descent, Sal, as everyone called him, was from one of the many Italian families that had come to the Wallton area to work in the coal mines. Unlike many of his siblings, Sal had completed high school, worked only a couple of years in the mines, and when a job as deputy came open, he had applied and been accepted.

"Bet November's gonna be a real killer . . . like a couple of years ago," Musso added, pushing a lock of black hair out of eyes so blue they mimicked a cloudless summer sky. "Remember that one? Had over a foot of snow two weeks before Halloween."

Taylor nodded. He did remember. That much snow had been totally unexpected so early in the year. Usually Wallton could count on a couple of light snows in November and early December and a fairly heavy one the week before Christmas. School vacation would have started by that time, and kids would be out tromping around, building snowmen, having snowball fights. Some of the older boys could earn a little money shoveling porches and sidewalks for older people, particularly widows.

"Yeh," Taylor said. "I remember that we went and checked on some people living just outside of town. Made sure they had food, oil for their lamps and coal or wood for their stoves. Too bad they can't get electricity out there." He stopped speaking for a minute and then continued. "Now that I think of it, I'd better take a look and see whether we need coal here and at home. Better stock up as we know the weather will only get worse for the next couple of months."

"Worse until May you mean," Musso grunted. "We've even had some bad snows in May."

"Well, the good side of bad weather is that it seems to cut down on our workload. People don't seem to get out as much. I know for a fact that we have a great deal less theft in the winter."

"Must be because everyone has their place locked up tight," Musso responded and headed for the door. "Gonna take a run around the town, just to see if everything is okay. Don't want trouble like we had this past summer."

No, I don't want any more trouble like we had last summer. Don't know how to stop something like that before it happens. Don't know how to recognize someone who's gonna do something like that. Just can't believe it could happen again.

Taylor rubbed his forehead, feeling the tension and the beginning of a headache. Unfortunately, the $500 reward that banker Allen offered had brought in no significant information. As was to be expected, numerous individuals had called or come by the office to tell of seeing someone in their neighborhood who they didn't recognize. Two women said that the day the Gower child was found a hobo had stopped by their doors asking for food, but the descriptions of the men provided by the women varied widely.

One individual reported that she had seen the retarded son of a neighbor outside the day of the murder and that the boy could be violent at times; however, when Allen spoke with the mother, she immediately became infuriated and blamed a neighbor for accusing her son. Apparently the boy had been in bed ill on that specific day, and when Taylor checked with Dr. Mason, he confirmed the boy's illness. Everyone was interested in the bank's $500 reward offer, but no one provided anything that helped the investigation move forward. Eventually, Jenifer Gower's death was relegated to the background when other law enforcement and other public issues, most of a minor nature, had to be handled.

As Deputy Musso had predicted, snow came to Wallton the middle of November, but it was chiefly scattered flurries and melted fairly quickly. Then, the week after Thanksgiving, more than six inches of the white stuff fell in a little over four hours. Still the main highway through town was open as that snow quickly melted off the bitumen. On the other hand, the side streets, mostly gravel, remained difficult to get through on foot or in a car. However, most of Wallton's population were accustomed to walking to jobs or stores and simply donned heavy coats, buckled on snow shoes, and went about their business. Snowmen, complete with coal for eyes, appeared in several yards, and snowball fights, especially among boys, were a great form of entertainment as children made their way to and from school.

Two more light snowstorms in December heaped another few inches of fluff atop a crust of earlier snow which had melted somewhat and formed a thin layer of ice underneath. Afraid of slipping, people could be seen gingerly making their way up Main Street, many using some form of cane or holding on to buildings for support. Taylor's crew all had been issued galoshes with heavy rubber soles in a pattern that would let them move freely with only a minimum fear of falling.

"Do not go out," Taylor had warned his mother. "If we need something from the grocers, I'll get it. Do not go out!"

"What about church?" Mrs. Taylor asked. "You know someone has to play the music."

Taylor agreed. He knew that his mother looked forward to Sundays and the camaraderie of her church friends. Every Sunday morning Nell Taylor played the organ for the choir. Although Nell had never had formal lessons, she could "play by ear" as the saying went. She had a small cadre of religious music that she played fairly well, including the usual old favorites, *Rock of Ages, Abide with Me, I Go to the Garden Alone,* and the Methodist congregation's favorite, *Onward Christian Soldiers.*

"Don't worry. I'll get you to church. Do not go out today on the slick streets," Taylor repeated as he opened their front door and felt a blast of icy air rush into his lungs. He was well aware that Nell Taylor would agree with his instruction and then do what she wished. "Promise me that you won't go out in this snow to run some silly errand."

Taylor sighed. At least the winter weather tended to keep most people inside their homes, including those who might cause some sort of trouble for him and his men.

<hr />

While the snow could be an inconvenience for most travel, it did not keep Santa from coming to Wallton. On Christmas Eve, families with children were bundled up and waiting in front of the train depot. Excitement was high among those young enough to still believe in Santa Claus, and questions like "Where is he?" and "Why's it taking so long?" could be heard above the murmur of adult voices as neighbors discussed the high cost of fuel and food or the fear of a possible loss of employment. Mixed in were the stamping of shoes to try and keep feet warm and an occasional voice directing a child to "Keep those mittens on; do you hear me!"

A rumble was detected as the train, much shorter in length than a normal one, slowly made its way to the depot. Stepping down from the last car was Santa, his red and white costume lit by the car's windows. A shriek of delight could be heard in the children's voices as Santa made his way toward the waiting group and handed out a wrapped parcel and a small bag of candy to each child, the largesse supposedly paid for by Wallton's First National Bank.

I recall dad and mom bringing me in to see Santa when I was six or seven, Taylor recalled, *even though sometimes it was hard getting through the snow drifts and back to the ranch. I think mom also enjoyed it. If she didn't, she never complained.*

He watched the delight in some of the children's eyes and knew for many that this might be their only Christmas gift as the economy showed little sign of getting better. Those families lucky enough to have someone employed could not use the meager wages frivolously. Actually the funds to purchase Santa's gifts for the youngsters had come directly from banker Allen and his sister although neither of the Allens were present to watch the festivities. Taylor tried to remember if the two individuals had ever attended the annual event but could not recall seeing either of them.

Both the station's tiny waiting room and a nearby pinon tree had been decorated with several strings of colored lights which added to the festivities. Around town, Taylor had seen several businesses with a small tree or lights and tinsel in their windows. The bank placed a large Spruce inside its entry and a wreath of holly on one of the doors. J. C. Penney's had a large tree decorated with red, gold and green lights in one of its two display windows, and this drew a number of young children along the front of the store close to five o'clock every evening. It would begin to get dark around 4:30 p.m., and as night closed in, they would disperse and hurry home for the evening meal since most families in Wallton ate supper between five-thirty and six o'clock.

As Santa climbed back aboard the train, it slowly moved away, and the crowd broke up. The temperature was dropping, a brisk wind had come up, and everyone was eager to get home. Taylor could hear voices commenting on the penetrating cold, particularly those of the smaller children who clung close to their parents for warmth. He noticed that some did not wear galoshes, and one boy's shoes were ripped in the back.

Probably outgrown them and family has no money to buy more or get them fixed. No socks either. His feet must be frozen. Hope this is not an upcoming case of pneumonia for Doc Mason.

Taylor shrugged. He could do nothing to remedy the situation. There were probably several kids in Wallton who did not have adequate shoes and socks. It was time for him to get home and get warm. He'd mention the nearly shoeless boy to his mother. Maybe she'd know if the church or some other group could help out the family. However, he suddenly realized that he didn't know the name of that particular family and wondered if they had just moved to Wallton or lived outside the town, maybe at one of the coal camps.

For New Year's Eve, Taylor's mother had invited a large number of people to spend the evening at their home. Nell Taylor was famous for her eggnog which she whipped up "from scratch," beating egg yolks until they were pale yellow and froth and adding the egg whites which had been whipped into fluffy peaks. Finally she dropped in "just a bit of whiskey." Taylor's mother did not approve of "spirits" and only used whiskey at the New Year gathering or for cough syrup which she made herself – a little whiskey, sugar, a bit of water and a drop of turpentine. As long as Abel Taylor could remember, he and his father had been made to take this remedy whenever they had a cough or "felt a cold coming on."

In addition to the egg nog there were coffee, tea and hot cider spiced with cinnamon. To make room for everyone the dining room table had been pushed against one wall and was laden with miniature sandwiches, various shelled nuts, cakes, pies, and a multitude of Christmas cookies decorated with red and green frosting. No one would leave hungry or thirsty from Nell Taylor's home.

Taylor knew or briefly had met all of his mother's guests, most of the people near her age and from her church, quilting group, the Eastern Star, or the Masonic Lodge. He also knew that she expected him to greet each of the guests and exchange a few words. This particular evening he was surprised, and a bit annoyed, to see that among the people her age she had included two young females.

Agnes Parsons, the twenty-year-old daughter of the new pastor, stood talking quietly with his mother. In early November Reverend Gower had asked the church elders to be reassigned to another parsonage away from Wallton, hoping that the change would benefit his wife. Julia Gower continued to be subject to depression and uncontrolled spells of weeping over the death of her daughter, and it was felt by her husband that a new and distant town in Kansas might help ease her anguish. For the Wallton church members, having the new Reverend Frederick Parsons, his daughter, and his wife, Annabelle, helped them forget the past summer's tragedy.

Dressed in a red wool dress and a single strand of pearls, Agnes Parsons certainly presented a fashionable picture of the holidays. Slender, with dark brown eyes and curly hair that was nearly black, she smiled graciously at Taylor as he greeted her.

"Are you getting used to Wallton, Miss Parsons?" Taylor asked.

"Please call me Agnes, she replied smiling. "Everyone does."

He knew nothing about the woman, had only heard his mother say that the Parsons had a daughter, "a marriageable daughter" was what he remembered her saying. Taylor was glad when Agnes took over the conversation, relieving him of groping for a topic. She took some time explaining that she had taught school for a year before her family moved. Just the past month she had been hired as a substitute teacher at Wallton's grade school. She laughed when she mentioned that she was very aware that people made a joke of her father's name, referring to him as "Parson Parsons." As they chatted, Taylor glanced at his mother and saw her watching him and smiling slightly.

No you don't, mom. I know you want me to get married, but I'm not going to get seriously mixed up with just anyone who is available and certainly not with someone churchy. You can keep pushing, and I'll just keep backing away . . . a long, long way back.

Explaining to Agnes Parsons that he needed to circulate among the other guests, Taylor slowly made his way around the room, chatting for a few minutes with each person. Eventually he ended up next to Barbara Hershey whom he had not seen since his meeting with George Allen at the bank and who seemed to be alone at the gathering. He noted that her blonde hair was not pinned back severely, as he had seen it when she was at work. Now it lay in soft waves around her face and made her look considerably younger than he remembered. Marcelled he thought the women called that hair style. Barbara also appeared much prettier than he remembered; yet the dark gray dress she had on did nothing to liven her pale skin even though she had lightly dusted her cheeks with rouge.

"Busy at the bank?" he asked, hoping that the comment would lead to Agnes taking over the brunt of the conversation.

"Not too busy. Money is scarce these days so not many making deposits," she answered briefly, leaving Taylor to grasp for another topic.

"I seem to remember you from school, although you were quite a ways behind me," Taylor commented.

"I suppose you could call it quite a ways. You were finishing at the high school, and I was just finishing sixth grade. We were never actually in school together, if that's what you mean."

"My mistake," Taylor replied. "I guess I didn't think I was so much older than you." He realized that he was fumbling for words and knew that she was aware of his discomfort.

"Not too much older; maybe six years or a little more. That doesn't make you ancient."

"Not really, I guess," He fumbled for a response, not knowing what the woman expected him to say.

Darn mother. She knows I don't know much about handling women, and she constantly puts me in these situations. I like women, but I just never seem to know what to say to them. Never have known.

When he had come into town for high school, Taylor had "taken a fancy" as it was put in those days to a girl in his class who had dark brown eyes and brunette hair usually tied away from her face with a blue or pink ribbon. Since Abel always needed to leave Wallton right after classes for his chores around the ranch, his interest never came to much. He was able to exchange only a few words with her from time to time at a few school functions and during graduation parties. A few months after graduation, he had heard that she married a man from a city to the north, a friend of her family.

Three years later he had taken the job as a deputy and had become friends with another young woman, actually a little more than friends, and had contemplated the idea of eventually asking her to marry him. Small in stature with hair the color of rust and penetrating blue eyes, Hazel Stone (or "Haze" as her friends called her) came from a "good family" and was considered a "good catch," whatever that meant. Her family liked Taylor; his mother liked Hazel and had mentioned frequently that she would be an excellent wife.

"Having a wife gives you stability," she had explained. "Makes people know you are committed to your job and the town."

Yet he could not bring himself to make a commitment to someone for the rest of his life; the relationship cooled and finally stalled. Eventually Hazel had met and married a local man who had a stable job as weigher at one of the nearby coal mines.

To end his uncomfortable conversation with Barbara Hershey, Taylor merely asked if she needed more egg nog and when she didn't, he excused himself to go and get himself a refill. As he was reaching for the eggnog ladle, he heard a knock at the front door and assumed it was an additional guest; however, it turned out to be one of his deputies, the one who had the bad luck to be on duty New Year's Eve.

"Sorry, Sheriff," Deputy Max Edson began, as Taylor approached. He hastily took off his hat, revealing neatly trimmed straw-colored hair. Shivering slightly, he glanced around the room at the gathering and spoke low enough that he couldn't be heard by anyone standing nearby.

"We've had a bit of trouble. One guy, you know Ernesto from out on the old Warren place, was fooling with his pistol. He wanted to shoot it off at midnight to celebrate the beginning of 1935 but shot himself in the foot instead. I took him up to the hospital and called Doc Mason, but no one answered. Don't know if Doc would keep him in or send him home."

Taylor explained to Edson that Mason had not answered his phone because he was a guest at the party. Then he considered what the deputy had said. The hospital, as it was called, was quite small and fairly old. Babies could be born there although most were born at home. It was equipped to handle pneumonia cases if there weren't too many at one time, but surgery, unless it was a matter of life or death, was always done at hospitals to the north. However, Taylor supposed Mason might keep the injured man the rest of the night, but he knew there would be only one nurse available on New Year's Eve. She would have to handle any patients unlucky enough to be hospitalized over the holiday. He caught the doctor's eye from across the room and signaled the man to join him and the deputy.

"Don't worry about the guy with the foot," Taylor said. "Doc will take a look at it. Everything else all right?"

"No, Sir!" Edson emphasized the last word. He was relatively new on the staff, having been hired about eleven months earlier, and took his job as deputy seriously. "Couple of guys were drinking, got in a really nasty fight. Both beat up pretty bad and bleeding quite a bit. I had to arrest them just to keep them apart. I've put them in jail. Separated them in two cells. Sorry to bring you all this." The deputy looked around at the Taylor's guests who had stopped chatting and were listening intently as they tried to catch the latest police news.

"Nothing to worry about; just the usual problems, but I'd better go check out the situation," Taylor answered, nodding to his mother and the other guests and beckoning the doctor toward the door.

"We need you, doc," he explained as Mason joined him and Edson.

The two men donned coats, hats and gloves and the three went out, hurriedly shutting the door against the freezing temperature. Taylor hoped the two men arrested would be the only persons needing to be jailed that night. Wallton's jail consisted of only three small cells, and most of the time one of those was utilized as a storage area for coal.

As the three drove away in separate cars, Taylor couldn't help smiling to himself. *Saved by the bell. Wasn't particularly looking forward to going out in the frigid night, but at least this keeps me from fumbling around for conversation with those two young women. Gonna have to have a serious talk with mom. She's bound and determined to get me hitched up. Wonder which of the two she would prefer to have as a daughter-in-law.*

———————•◦◆◦•———————

Winter finally settled hard on Wallton. A blizzard struck the town in early February, just in time for Groundhog Day. Beginning with strong winds which howled around houses and down streets, over two feet of snow fell during one afternoon and into the night, breaking tree limbs and threatening power lines. Those who had automobiles found it impossible to navigate accumulated drifts, and Taylor did not even try. Making certain that he was adequately clothed against the cold, shortly after seven o'clock in the morning he struggled to the office, nearly falling on his face in the snow as he stepped from a curb. Still, all in all, it was a nice day. The snow had stopped, the air was crisp, the sun shone brightly in a pale blue sky, and long icicles glistened from the eaves of buildings.

The highway connecting the town to other parts of the state lay pristine under a white blanket. No traffic was visible, and Taylor wondered if nearby towns were in the same shape as Wallton. *Got to do something about the road* he thought as he inserted his key into the lock on the front door and went into his office.

The telephone was ringing, but Taylor ignored it. It was probably a call for help, but there was little he could do to help anyone. He was glad to know that at least one of Wallton's three telephone operators was on the job and wondered how the woman had been able to get to work. *Maybe she stayed all night. If that's true, it's certainly dedication, and I'll need to make sure people know about it.*

Getting a shovel from a storage area, he began shoveling the sidewalk in front of the building and around the corner to Main Street. Although the snow was deep, it was fairly light and flaky, and he made good progress. From down Main he heard a call and saw Deputy Musso stumbling toward him through the drifts.

"What a damn mess," Musso panted as he reached the corner. "Anyone else here but you and me?"

"No, but I'm sure all of our men will be here soon as they can make their way. Going to need all the help we can get."

"What we gonna do about the road?" Musso pointed to the expanse of snow stretching from the south to the north end of town. A small elevation existed at both ends of Wallton, and the men could see an outline of the big "W" hovering over a hill on the south end. It had been constructed of large stones nearly ten years earlier, and each year the stones were re-painted white by Wallton high school students. Now covered with snow and a bit of haze, the "W" was nearly invisible.

"I'll start calling any citizens who have telephones – asking those strong enough to do some heavy work to join us – and you go see if you can round up a few close to here. We'll need to do a lot of shoveling. Have the men bring their own equipment, and tell them they'll probably be needed for several hours, maybe the whole day. Don't want their wives mad."

Musso started off to the south end of town, and Taylor began his calls. Within an hour, in addition to the eight deputies, over twenty citizens carrying snow shovels had made their way to the office. Working steadily, by a little after three o'clock they were able to clear a seven-foot-wide path down the center of the town from the hill at the north end to the hill at the south end.

"That's it," Taylor said to the exhausted men as they leaned on their shovel handles or supported themselves against building walls. "If someone needs to drive today in case of an emergency, he can make it up or down one way where we've shoveled. Can't pass each other, but if people are fool enough to come out, they will just have to wait their turn."

"Haven't seen a car since we've been working, Sheriff," lawyer Sam Browning said. "None coming through from out of town. Few people out but not too many, and all are walking. The drugstore's open in case someone needs medicine, and I saw a couple of guys going into Willard's Cafe. Guess people have to eat, especially some of the single guys who live at the hotel."

Taylor nodded. "He knew Browning was referring to the town's Central Hotel, a two-story structure with a lobby, a bar and seven upstairs rooms. "Well, at least we won't have too many people committing crimes today. Can't get out and about as usual."

He thanked the citizens for all of their help and watched as they began to trudge off home, shovels slung over aching shoulders. Already the afternoon sun had begun to melt the drifts from the top, packing the moisture down which would make it harder to move. Entering his office, Taylor plopped down at his desk and sat for a few minutes ignoring the ringing telephone. Deputy Ted Michaels had followed Taylor into the building and took the call.

"Emergency?" Taylor asked.

"No, just asking what we are going to do about all of the snow," Michaels answered. "Wonder if people think we're magicians and can just wave a magic wand, and summer will be here." The deputy, a stocky bald man in his early forties, shook his head as if to indicate that he couldn't understand people asking stupid questions. "I told him we were working on it."

———◆———

'Think I'll take a stroll up to Doc Mason's office, "Taylor said to Alma one afternoon in early April, the cottonwood trees just beginning to show a hint of green leaves. "Talk with him again about the Gower girl's death."

"Why? He don't know any more than he did when it happened." Alma responded bluntly, looking up from her desk. "Just a waste of your time, and it'll just get you all stirred up again."

"You're probably right, Alma, but you never know. Might be something he thought about afterwards. At any rate, it'll put my mind at ease somewhat." Taylor put on his hat and a light jacket. "It's fairly nice out today, but the wind's come up. You know where to get me if you need me."

Alma's like my mother. Always giving me advice, but she's right. Doc isn't going to know any more than I do, and that's next to nothing. Guess I just needed to get out of the office for a spell. Hope Doc isn't so busy that he can't spend a few minutes with me. Change in the weather always brings about a lot of people with colds, maybe even the flu so know there'll be patients, always is.

The last thought made Taylor shake his head. He could remember what everyone referred to as the "bad flu season" which actually had lasted almost five years into the early 1920s. It had been a year or two before his graduation from high school. Seemed like almost everyone was sick. Whole families were sick. Some lost two or three members of their family to the illness.

When he entered Mason's office, he found several patients anxiously waiting to see the doctor and nodded to those he recognized. Indicating nothing was urgent and that he was in no hurry, he picked up a copy of the past week's newspaper and sat down near the door. He had already seen most items of interest from the paper but didn't wish to get involved in conversation with the other people.

Nearly two hours elapsed before the physician appeared and ushered Taylor back to his cramped office. It was just as Taylor remembered it, but the doctor appeared to have changed somewhat over the past months since their late evening talk in the garden. His hair, which he always made certain was neatly combed with a side part on the left, showed a few more traces of gray, and Taylor thought a couple of additional creases had etched themselves in his forehead.

Wonder how old he is? I've never asked and don't intend to, but he doesn't look too well himself . . . certainly looks tired. What if something were to happen to him? Except for the two who look after the miners and live at the company towns, there are no other doctors for at least forty miles, and I'll bet the mine docs have their hands full. How'd we get another doctor, especially one to come to this small town? Lot of hard work and not much reward for a doctor in a town the size of Wallton.

"You sick or just looking for some company?" Mason asked gruffly.

"Sorry," Taylor began and smiled at the older man. "I know you're really busy, Doc. I hate to bother you, but do you remember a boy's death a few years ago? Think his name was Robert Wilson."

"Yeah, I may recall something." Mason stopped talking and rubbed his hand over his head, smoothing his already smooth hair. Suddenly he said, "Now I remember. He was about twelve or close to that age. David Stanton Wilson. I remember the name as it seemed way too long for a boy. Stanton must have been his mother's maiden name. His folks called him 'Davy,' not David. His mother particularly. Handsome little boy with very light brown, almost blonde, curly hair. That's been three or four years ago. Could be a bit longer. My memory's not so good these days. Killed up by the railroad tracks. Wasn't found 'til fairly late in the evening, almost dark."

"Do you recall what killed him?"

"Blow to the head I think. Thought it had been caused by a chunk of coal since there was some coal residue around the wound. Loaded coal cars are all the time losing chunks. You know that. Slab dropping from a car could do a lot of damage to anyone. Kid playing right near the tracks. Not surprising that he got hit in the head. Accidents happen, you know?"

"Yeh, accidents happen," Taylor acknowledged. "You didn't think it could have been something other than an accident?"

A puzzled look came over Mason's face. Stretching, he rubbed the back of his neck and peered closely at Taylor. "You think it was something else? Think I might have missed something?"

"No. no!" Taylor was quick to reassure the older man. "The Gower girl's death just got me to thinking about any children who've died recently. Other than those who died from some kind of illness."

"Well the Wilson boy wasn't all that recent. I can look up my records if you've got the time." Mason stood and slowly made his way to a filing cabinet, its wooden drawers scarred and sagging with the weight of too many folders. "Sure it's here somewhere unless we've already stored it in the attic."

Been only about a year since we found the Gower child, but just can't get over how Doc seems to have aged since then, and he's limping a little. I don't recall that he had a limp. Wonder if he hurt himself somehow. Maybe had a fall. I'd ask, but it would just upset him and . . .

"Here it is. Knew it had to be somewhere." Mason grumbled. Moving back to his seat, the doctor opened the file and began to read.

"Yep, just as I said. Laceration on the scalp. Something heavy that cut right into the brain. Kid might not have died if someone had found him sooner. My conclusion was that the head injury was the cause of his death, probably caused by a very large lump of coal that lay nearby and had some blood on it. Nothing much else found around him but smaller pieces of coal."

Mason closed the folder and peered at Taylor. "Why you asking about this? You heard something different?"

"No, no. Just thinking. Just trying to look at any other kids who have died. Except, of course, from some disease or an accident that someone saw happen. Course you'd think if someone saw this one happen, they'd have helped out or called someone."

Mason nodded his head and then said, "Well, it was unusual . . . a kid dying like that. Course we still lose children occasionally from diphtheria or scarlet fever. Lost one and a mother from smallpox a few years ago. That's still around although people can be vaccinated against the pox if they'd just take the time to do so, but you know how people are . . ."

"Town people?" Taylor interrupted. He knew the disease could be deadly. Even if people recovered, they were usually scarred for life. He thought of a boy in his high school classes who had pits on his face.

"No, that smallpox was on a ranch out in the county. Actually it wasn't much of a ranch. No cattle to speak of and a wretched adobe house with three rooms. I vaccinated the dad and the other five kids. None of them came down with the disease although the dad was quite sick for a few days. Think I caught him just in time." Mason shook his head. "Don't know what they all did with the mother gone." He paused a moment and then continued. "Lose most of them in the county; they don't come in for help until it's too late. Need to get everyone vaccinated, but . . ." Mason stopped talking.

Taylor waited a few minutes before speaking again. "So, no other kids dying young from accidents?" He wanted to get Mason back to thinking about accidental deaths. "I seem to recall another boy who died about the time I began work as a deputy."

"Think you may be right," Mason replied as he closed the file folder. "What? Ten, twelve years ago? Can't remember much about the incident." He paused momentarily and then continued. "Seems to me there was even another one about seven years ago. Little boy . . . very dark hair as I recall . . . almost black. Can't recall names though. Just another autopsy . . . Don't know how you'll find out about them, even if I'm right."

"Might go take a look at past issues of the *Wallton Weekly*." Taylor stood up. "Sure there was something in the paper about the death. Just bothers me that I can't seem to find out any reason why someone would have killed the little Gower girl. I do appreciate you taking all this time to talk with me, Doc, as I could tell by the waiting room that you are swamped."

"Anytime, anytime," Mason replied as he got up from his desk and walked to the office door with Taylor. "Let me know if you come up with something, especially if it's something I missed. I'm not perfect, you know, but I don't think I miss much so don't think you're going to find anything except what's in this file." He handed the folder to Taylor. "You read it. Might be of some help to you. Take it with you, but be sure to get it back to me, you hear!"

———•◆•———

As he had indicated to the doctor, Taylor walked to the newspaper office and explained to the owner and publisher that he wished to check an issue from several years previously although he wasn't certain of the exact date. Cautioning him to watch his step, Mel Dawson took him down to a small cellar where huge black binders containing past copies of the daily were stored. Taylor could see that the binders were stacked almost ceiling high.

"How many years are here?" Taylor asked as Dawson pulled the cord on a light hanging from the ceiling. The bulb covered with grit barely made a dent in the gloom.

"Don't know for sure," Dawson answered. "Think there may be copies from when the first edition came out . . . before my time . . . when the Stoddard family owned the paper. May be two years in each binder, at least two years, maybe more. Some issues are in old boxes over in the corner. You'll just have to rat around until you find the box or binder you need. Those over the last ten to twenty years are probably against that far wall. Take all the time you need. I got to get back out front." He started up the stairs and then hesitated. "Better keep your jacket on as it's damp down here. Don't want to catch cold. Oh, sorry about all the dirt and dust."

Dust there was. A thin layer coated every binder and seemed to permeate every corner of the small room, causing Taylor to sneeze several times. He brushed a large cobweb away from his face and began opening some of the binders and checking newspaper dates as he knew approximately the months he wanted. It was slow going, leafing through the pages and scanning each one. Some of the pages had articles clipped from them, and he hoped those would not be the articles he wished to read.

Nearly three hours passed before Taylor found when the second boy that he mentioned to Mason had been killed. There wasn't much of a story, just a few inches of type on the bottom of the November front page indicating that the boy, Carlos Hernandez, had been found close to dusk by a railroad worker, pronounced dead by the coroner, and that an accident was the reason for the death. Taylor also found the boy's brief obituary which only listed the usual funeral information – surviving kin, time of services, place of burial. What was not in the newspaper was any mention of the type of accident which Taylor found interesting. Had the boy been hit by one of the loaded cars? Had he stumbled under a car?

Probably was just an accident, Taylor sneezed as he bent over the article, blowing dust across the page. *Kid playing too close to the tracks or maybe he wasn't just playing. Maybe he was picking up any coal chunks that fell off the cars to be used for fuel at home. Coal's not cheap. Maybe he was just trying to help his family by bringing home several chunks of coal for the coming winter, and one fell off and hit him. Of course maybe he was just playing . . . trying to hop on one of the cars for a bit of a ride . . . car moving too fast . . .?*

Taylor knew he was simply guessing about the cause of the accident. Yet he continued to leaf through the old newspaper, hoping for more information. All he found of any interest was an editorial warning parents that they should keep their children away from the railroad tracks.

A useless warning. Nothin' more fascinating to a boy than a train unless it's the creek. Boys? Never heard much about girls being near the tracks or down at the creek for that matter. Was Jennifer Gower the only girl who had died, been murdered, in the past few years?

Taylor shook his head. Obviously the newspaper's brief story on Carlos Hernandez was of little help. He knew that a deputy would have been called when the boy was found and wondered whether the deputy would remember much or whether his report would mention if coal was scattered about the dead boy. The brief newspaper information bothered him. He would find out who the deputy was and, if the man were still working for the sheriff's department, see what he might recall. He knew that it was a long shot; still, a person didn't forget easily if he had been summoned to look at a dead body even if he was in a job where dead bodies occasionally turned up.

That night at dinner, he mentioned the earlier case. "Mother, do you recall that a boy was found dead a few years ago? Up by the tracks?"

"I think I remember," she replied after a few seconds. "The little Wilson boy. The couple's only son . . . had two daughters but the only boy.

"No, another boy a few years before that?"

"Oh, you must mean the Mexican boy from down by the Fair Grounds. Tenth Street, I think it was. Or maybe even further down – just before you reach the creek." She looked at her son. "Why? Do you think it's connected to the little Gower girl's death? I thought the Wilson' boy's death was just an accident, and Jennifer was found in the creek . . . not anywhere near the trains."

"No, No!" Taylor began hastily. "Nothing to do with Jennifer Gower. Just thinking about other young people who've died." He didn't want his mother getting too interested and pressing him for more details about the dead boy or the lack of progress being made on Jennifer Gower. Still, he was amazed at how easily his mother recalled the information he needed and wondered if it was just because it involved the death of someone young.

Nothing more interesting than death . . . unless it's the Depression. Guess both are the most terrible things that affect people right now.

"I'm sure the boy's death was just an accident," his mother continued, "but you do recollect another little boy who was killed way before that? Not long after we moved into town. Just can't recall his name right now. His family didn't belong to our church. You'd only been a deputy for a bit, and I don't think you had much to do with that death?"

Now, Taylor vaguely remembered, although if his mother had not brought up the incident, he might not have. He'd been working as a deputy for several years then, but for some reason which he could not remember, another more experienced deputy and Sheriff Brown had handled the incident. He couldn't remember who the deputy was but thought that man had moved away from Wallton. He could ask Alma the next morning as she had a fantastic memory when it had anything to do with the office. Then again that might not be a good idea. She'd wonder why he was curious, and he wasn't certain he didn't wish to explain his curiosity.

Just seems like there are too many young people dying from accidents in such a small town. Every few years or so . . . and with no one around when the supposed accident occurs. Wonder if kids are dying in the same way in other towns. Might take a look at even earlier editions of our newspaper when I have some time. See if there's any mention of young people accidentally dying in other towns around the state. That would be news even for the Wallton Weekly. Also, would give me some idea if there is a killer only in our midst. Then he remembered the newspaper's cellar and his last foray down there. *Hope I can stand all that dirt and dust again.*

There had been no further incidents of accidental death to young people since the Gower child's murder the previous year. At the middle of June, when school let out for the summer, the *Wallton Weekly* once again printed on its front page an article asking parents to warn their children about going to the creek. Because of the snowmelt from the nearby mountains, the creek was running unusually high, and a kid could easily slip, possibly hit his head on a rock and drown. The memory of the last summer's tragedy still lingered, and most parents heeded the warning, promising swift retribution if one of their offspring was found near the water.

"Well, I hope the warning does some good," Doctor Mason said to Taylor as the two ate a hurried lunch. "Still, the lure of the creek is mighty strong. I can remember going down there almost every summer day when I was young."

"The creek was there when you were young?" Taylor asked.

"Don't be a smart ass!" Mason snapped. "I may not be as young as you, but I'm still able to hold my own with the best of them." The doctor got up, told Taylor to pay the tab and headed out the door.

I hope he's right Taylor thought as he watched the man walk up Main Street. *We'd be in a lot of trouble if something happens to him. Medically speaking, he's the history of this town, actually the entire county. I should have asked him about that other boy's death . . . the one mother mentioned a while ago . . . but got to talking about other things . . . Got something else to do right now.*

Taylor paid $1.35 for the two lunches, left a dime for a tip, and spoke briefly to several people as he made his way to the door. Then he drove to the eastern outskirts of Wallton where members of a small circus were in the process of running a cable from a power pole for electricity needed to run a carousel of painted horses which young children particularly liked to ride. He could see that some of the bright paint was peeling from several of the animals, and a few were missing the tips of their ears.

Traveling in a caravan of old Ford trucks, the performers had arrived the previous afternoon, purchased a few supplies at a local grocery store, distributed flyers to anyone walking on the street, and added to the local bars' weekly income. Since the town and surrounding county had such a sparse population, it could not attract a major circus. Still, for as long as Taylor could remember, even during the war years, this same circus had stopped at Wallton before moving on east into small Kansas towns. For him and all of the other young people, that circus had been the highlight of their summer.

Although there were only a few incidents, mostly minor, where circus individuals had been involved with Wallton deputies, Taylor knew that the circus could bring problems for law enforcement. His staff was limited, and with almost everyone attending the festivities, he was very aware that businesses and homes would be good robbery targets for those who were not inclined to join the circus crowds. He also was aware that the booths set up to attract people to buy souvenirs and other trinkets handled shoddy merchandise with expensive prices. He also knew that those individuals, usually children, trying to win prizes at various games would most likely lose as the risk was rigged in favor of the vendors.

Particularly he recalled one vendor who had been able to set up a stream of water running over a counter in front of his tent. In the water an occasional fake fish would float by. If the player was lucky enough to grab the fish in a tiny net, a prize would be awarded. The cost to the player was ten cents for three attempts. Ten cents was a lot of money for a child in those days, and the prize, if forthcoming, was worth about a penny. Still, he remembered when, as a young boy, he had "fished." How happy he had been if he won a prize and how dejected if he lost.

"Mr. Lapize. I see nothing's changed," Taylor said as he shook the hand of Pieter Lapize, owner of *Wonders of the World*. The man was dressed in dusty corduroy trousers with a colorful long-sleeved shirt and black vest. "Still the same old circus."

"With exception of new clown we are yet as we was last year," the man replied in halting English. "Little new change."

Except you Taylor thought. *When did you become so stooped? I guess I hadn't thought about how old you are. Let's see. You must be past sixty now, probably nearing seventy. This constant traveling about the country must be hard on you.*

"Better make sure your animals are watered," Taylor said as he looked around the prairie where the trucks were parked and pointed in the direction of three horses and several dogs. He shook his head as he looked across the vacant ground at several men attempting to set up a tent for the night's performance, a slight wind causing its canvas to drag in the dirt.

This circus is not really a circus. When I was about eleven, dad took mom and me on the train to Denver for a stock show. At that same time, a circus was in the city – a circus with elephants and lions, a circus that held a big parade down one of the main streets. I got to see that parade. Got to go to that circus.

Somehow he felt a twinge of regret that most of Wallton's children would never see that kind of circus, never get to travel as he had since there would be little money. They would grow up, marry, have kids of their own, hopefully be able to work every day, grow old, die, and be buried in one of the town's two cemeteries. Many would probably never go further away than maybe forty or fifty miles and would consider those big trips.

"You be present tonight for the performance, Sheriff?" Lapize questioned formally, interrupting Taylor's thoughts.

"Plan to be," Taylor responded and then added, "and may bring a lady with me."

Until he made the statement, he had not planned on bringing anyone. The idea had just come to him. Walking around the circus with a woman, he could keep an eye on people with everyone thinking he was simply out for a good time. He would call and invite Agnes Parsons to accompany him. If she did not have other plans, he would be her escort for an evening at the circus. He smiled at the thought.

That should make mother happy. She can make certain all of her friends hear that her aging son is going out with a female. Soon the whole town will hear the news. Sheriff Taylor is out escorting a woman. Will wonders never cease!

———————•◆•———————

Labor Day weekend brought the flood. While the creek in August and September mostly had no more than a trickle of water, unusually heavy rainfall in the mountains over a three-day period caused a swift current to rush downslope into Wallton on a Sunday afternoon.

"Nearly four feet and rising," Musso reported to Taylor who had been in his office since dusk Sunday evening. "Bet it may get up to five or six feet before midnight. Drury told me it was higher than he'd seen it in quite a few years, and Arn's been around here a long time."

"I've called in everyone, even Alma. If it gets as high as you think, we've got to move families out of the low-lying south part of town. As soon as Alma gets here I'll have her call people we know have a car. If the water doesn't get too deep, most families can walk out, but some who are older or infirm can't. Also, we'll ask for help from those situated higher up, get people to try and load some of the belongings of those without any kind of transportation and who are sure to be flooded. Let's try and move their stuff to dry ground. Get deputies to drive through the streets honking the horn constantly. Get people alerted; Yell! Knock on doors if you have to. Get the people moving to dry ground!"

He had thought of telling the deputies to fire their guns to get citizens' attention but then had second thoughts. Although he and the other men were armed, they seldom had to use their weapons. Several times a year Taylor and the deputies went a few miles outside Wallton to an abandoned gravel pit and had firearm practice. However, it was so seldom that he didn't want to take the chance that in the anxiety to make everyone aware of the flood danger someone, a Wallton deputy or maybe even a resident, might be accidentally shot.

Within an hour, responding to Alma's frantic calls, the citizens of Wallton who had autos were on the street in front of the sheriff's office. Taylor stood on the hood of one of the cars, addressing the assembled men.

"Thanks for coming. My deputies are out warning the citizens and urging them to get to higher ground. Deputy Musso has just reported the creek is now over its banks, and water is already ankle deep clear up to Seventh Street and rising. We need to make sure everyone is out from their homes in the lower part of town. Go in pairs. Help anyone who is unable to walk."

"What if they won't go?" one man yelled.

"Just take them! Don't let them talk you into leaving them. Try to be gentle, nice . . . but if you can't, just get them to higher ground. Then go back if the water is not too deep and try to save some of their belongings. That's what I really need you to do. Try to save some of the furnishings, clothing. Most of the people in that part of town don't have much, and anything we can save will help them out later. I expect the water to get fairly high, and some of those houses sit at ground level without any foundation or even wooden floors. There's bound to be a lot of damage, but can't worry about that. Get the people out first! Belongings can be fixed; drowned people can't."

The men drove off, and Taylor returned to his desk. "Lots of calls, Sheriff," Alma reported. "People wondering what's happening and what they should do. I just told them to move out if they were below Seventh Street. Otherwise stay put in their home, but you know people. They all want to see what's happening, so people will be out everywhere, even though it's getting dark, and you can't see much of anything."

Yes, Taylor knew. It would be like the day after the little Gower girl was found. The bridge over the creek clogged with the curious, kids climbing up and down the creek sides. Everyone was interested in a tragedy unless they were one of the victims.

"Just do your best to encourage everyone out of the flood area to stay at home, Alma. It's all we can do. Maybe it won't be as bad as it looks now."

The water came and was gone in a few hours – a flash flood it was called by some. It had reached a little over five feet in depth in the lower part of town, and a few minor injuries were reported, but, luckily, no one was killed. The flood had simply swept into Wallton and swept out again, leaving behind piles of debris and a rotten stench that permeated the summer air.

For over forty families, their material loss was heavy. On the adobe houses particularly, water marks beginning to dry in the sun showed how high the water had reached. Surrounding yards of all of the homes were littered with bits of wet furniture and soggy mattresses as owners had attempted to save some household items before they had been forced to seek higher ground. In the Monday morning sunrise, their meager belongings lay saturated with mud, bedraggled bits of families' lives.

Taylor arrived home around nine o'clock Monday morning to get a bite to eat and stood on the front steps to remove his water-soaked boots and wet socks. Entering the house, he was surprised to find it filled with the noise of small children.

"The children were the first to be evacuated," his mother explained as she carried bowls of oatmeal to the kitchen able. Four girls somewhere between the ages of eight and ten began to add butter and sugar to their meal. His mother made sure the girls used the napkins she had provided and then scurried back to the stove.

"An uncle of the two over in that corner brought them up in his truck and went back to see if he could help others. Just left them by themselves." She shook her head annoyed by the man's actions. "They've been like that ever since they got here. Scared! Won't talk. Won't say who they are. They just sit there with the younger one clinging to the older girl's hand. Must be about five and six years old. I put that shawl over them to help them sleep as you know how chilly it can get in the morning hours."

Taylor merely nodded as he poured himself a cup of coffee from the percolator on the back of the stove. Watching his mother, he could see that in spite of her complaint, she was enjoying taking care of the girls.

Just like a mother or grandmother he thought and couldn't keep from smiling. *Busy, busy, busy. Taking care of someone young.*

Shortly after Taylor arrived home, the uncle of the two frightened girls came to pick them up. He thanked Taylor's mother for her care and said, "Still a big mess down there," as he pushed them toward the door and out toward his truck.

Taylor knew it was a big mess. In fact he knew that was an understatement. For many of Wallton's population, it was a catastrophe. After quickly eating a bowl of oatmeal and drinking two cups of coffee, he drove back to the south end of town and realized it would mean big trouble for weeks. Although the water had receded enough so that the creek appeared to be almost back to its normal flow, the stench rising from the mud and debris left by the flood would be around for days. Along with the sodden bedding dragged outside of homes, bits of furniture, its paint or varnish beginning to peel, gave off an acrid odor of paint thinner and turpentine.

The decaying half-eaten carcass of a doe, straddling a large bush, had been washed into town in the flood. Its odor caused him to gag, and he knew that he would have to get someone to remove the deer before dogs could get to it. There was also the fear that rattlesnakes, usually only found in the outlying county, would have been washed into town and lurked in hidden spots. A bite by a rattlesnake could be deadly.

Going to take several weeks to get back to anything like normal. He shook his head and watched as a large white cat scurried around the corner of a house, pursued by a young girl calling its name. *She doesn't seem to be upset by all the mess. Mother's right. In a short time, the flood will just be something to talk about and then forgotten until it happens again. Like the murder of the Gower child. Been a little over a year now, and it's no longer a topic of conversation. People forget quickly, especially some of the bad things. Unfortunately, I remember. I can't seem to get that killing out of my mind . . . just creeps in every now and then.*

Taylor watched the girl and her cat for another few minutes and then slowly drove back toward the office. There were a million things he would need to do – meet with the mayor, see if some place was being set up to feed those washed out of their houses, check with Mason to see if there had been any major injuries, release some of his deputies who had been on duty over eighteen hours. The list seemed endless. It was times like this that he considered giving up his job as sheriff and letting someone else worry about the town. But it was just a thought.

He figured he'd be the sheriff until he wasn't re-elected or until he died.

———◦◆◦———

"Going over to the newspaper, Alma," Taylor said shortly after noon on a cloudy November day. Grabbing his hat, he started toward the door. "Anyone needs me, they can find me there or you can call over."

"Be long, sheriff?" Alma asked, peering over the top of her glasses.

"Don't know. Could be quite a spell. Depends on what I find . . . or don't find."

He knew Alma was dying to ask why he was going again to the *Wallton Weekly* office, but he merely smiled at her and walked out the door.

"Problems, Sheriff," Mel Dawson asked as Taylor quickly closed the door to keep the cold breeze whipping up Main Street out of the newspaper's large front space. Even with the stove, a circulator it was called, pumping out hot air, the room with its two large windows facing the street felt chilly and damp. Dawson's gray-haired secretary Annie, a distant relative of his, was clad in a heavy sweater as she sat at her typewriter waiting for Dawson to finish the editorial he had been dictating to her. Joe Baines, Dawson's only other helper, was busy setting type for the next edition which would be available in two days.

"No, no! No problem that's newsworthy. Actually no problems at all. Just another usual day for which I am very grateful."

"So, what can I do for you then?"

"Well, do you remember that you said I could take another look at your back issues any time I wished to do so?"

"Sure, you know where they are. Remember there's no windows in that cellar, just the light, and the door's sticking a little, so you may have to put your back in it to get it to come up. Dawson shook his head. "Can't imagine what you are looking for or hoping to find."

"Don't know myself," Taylor replied, smiling. "Just want to see, maybe remember, how life was in Wallton when I was young."

"Best keep your things on," Annie cautioned. "It's bound to be a bit chilly down there."

Chilly was an understatement. He pulled the cord to the light and could see faintly his breath in the air. *Maybe not a good idea* Taylor thought as he pulled gloves off and stuffed them in his pocket. *Maybe I ought to wait 'til summer to leaf through all of this old newsprint.*

However, he was already in the cellar, and he wished to see if he could get more on the story that he had heard from his mother about another dead child. He couldn't explain it, even to himself. It wasn't just about Jennifer Gower although occasionally her death crept into his thoughts. He just couldn't seem to stop thinking that Wallton had too many deaths of children in accidents – accidents that could not be fully explained or at least had not been explained to his satisfaction. Blowing on his fingers, he toted a heavy book to a rickety table, blew dust from its cover, and began his search. He needed to take time and slowly look through editions at least ten years earlier.

After several hours of scanning the old pages, Taylor finally found what he was looking for – a small article from April, 1926. His mother had been right. A boy, Emilio Sanchez, had been found around dusk lying face down in a ditch about two blocks from his home. The newspaper article stated that there had been an especially heavy rain during the late afternoon of that day, and it was felt that while playing in the water, the boy had slipped on the muddy bank, fell face down, was unable to drag himself out of the water and had drowned. According to the article, the body was coated with mud and other bits of debris that had washed into the ditch and lodged in the depression. The conclusion was that the boy had been unable to drag himself out of the water as the sides were too slippery.

Wonder who found him . . . his parents, other kids . . . Wonder if he tried to call for help. Probably no one would have heard him if he did. Wonder if he was playing by himself. Must have been . . .

Immediately, Taylor began to leaf forward through the pages, looking for an obituary. As with the boy who had died from the chunk of coal, there was a brief one listing the boy's date of birth, surviving family and time of services at the Catholic Church. It would appear to be an ordinary accident, but something bothered Taylor.

He was eight years old, almost nine. He wasn't just a small child like Jennifer Gower. He should have been able to get out of that ditch unless he hit his head on something. The newspaper stories don't mention any wounds. It all seems too simple an explanation.

Taylor stuck a slip of paper between the pages he had been reading and looked several pages forward from the Sanchez boy's death in case he had missed something. He wasn't sure what he was hoping to find – a further mention of the tragedy perhaps. There was nothing.

Got to be more than just what's in the newspaper. Wonder if it was Doc Mason who got that case. Hope it was since old doctor McKenna has been dead for years now and doubt if his records were kept by the family. Don't even know if any of his family are still in Wallton. Think I'll run by in a couple of days and see if Mason remembers anything about this. Hate to keep pestering the Doc, but unless I can locate something or somebody else to talk with, he's my sole source of information.

Taylor carefully closed the huge book but left it on the table. He might want to leaf through it again although his common sense told him that in those pages he had already found anything there was to find.

Nevertheless, it would be several months before Taylor was able to find time for a meeting with Dr. Mason, and his interest in the boy's accidental drowning faded from his mind. First, Taylor once again had been invited to attend the semi-annual conference of Colorado Sheriffs in Denver. Since he had missed the last two, he decided to go. The four-day conference was held at Denver's Brown Palace, but, since Taylor's budget was limited, he and several other sheriffs from the smaller towns found less expensive lodgings at other nearby hotels.

Then the Thanksgiving, Christmas and New Year's holidays descended upon Wallton bringing not only inclement weather but the usual round of festivities. Taylor was invited to all of them and always made the effort to at least show up for a brief time. This year, he was able to avoid his mother's usual New Year's party by taking his turn at keeping someone on duty that night.

"It's got to be me," he had patiently explained to his mother. "I know I'm the boss, but all of my men have taken a turn at being available during the holidays. That includes the night shift. Now nothing may happen of any importance, usually doesn't, but just in case . . . You understand?"

Nell Taylor had nodded her agreement, but Taylor could see that she was very disappointed. She had mentioned that several young people would certainly be there, and by young he assumed she meant someone closer to his age. She also added that he didn't get to meet young people all that often as he usually saw only those who were in some kind of trouble. Taylor knew by the emphasis on the term young that she was referring to Agnes Parsons and Barbara Hershey.

He had asked Agnes out three times after their evening at the circus, once on a picnic in nearby mountains. once to hear a local dance band, and one to a movie. At her request, they had gone to see *King Kong*, but it seemed to Taylor that the couple were more interesting to the other attendees than the huge ape causing havoc on the screen. People seated in front of them casually would adjust a wrap or a collar as they sneaked a look at the couple. He could hear whispers behind them and wondered if all people went through the same thing when they were single and out on a date. *Maybe it's just the two of us . . . or maybe just me.*

Perhaps it was the way he was dressed that caused all of the interest. Since he would not be on duty that evening and because he thought Agnes might be more comfortable, he had not worn his uniform. The navy serge jacket had felt too small when he donned it as had the trousers, and he had spent some time trying to decide which of his two ties went best with his light blue shirt. The couple were obviously of more interest than what was on the screen.

Wonder if Agnes is as uncomfortable as I am with all of this covert attention. Old Sheriff Taylor out again with a woman. And the same woman!

Several times, at least three that he could recall, he had to telephone Agnes and explain that he could not keep their scheduled appointment. Taylor had also attempted to explain to both Agnes and his mother how irregular his job hours were.

"If something comes up, something that my guys think is urgent, I have to just drop what I'm doing or planning and go where the problem is. I know I try to keep regular hours for both myself and my deputies, but this doesn't always work out. So I don't always make it home for dinner or to an engagement, but that's just how it is . . . how it's got to be."

His mother had become accustomed to his duty commitments. However, he could tell that Agnes seemed not to hear nor understand his explanations. After he had canceled squiring her to a dance at the church, she had asked, actually almost demanded, a detailed explanation.

"There was an auto accident north of Wallton," Taylor had said. "Three women were returning from a visit to a friend on a nearby farm. I think they're church members so you probably know them. At any rate, the driver lost control of the vehicle, and it rolled over. One woman was pinned under part of the car, and when the two others tried to move, she would scream with pain as part of the auto pressed down on her. The three had been there for over two hours before they were discovered. I needed to go to the scene with one of my deputies and help get the women into Wallton."

"Oh, of course you had to be there," Agnes had replied hastily. "I know how important it is for you to help all of us when something bad happens. Still, it is disappointing that we can't plan things . . . and keep those plans. I'm certain your mother is upset when you can't get home sometimes for regular meals."

Taylor was aware that Agnes was only saying what was expected. He also had come to realize that they had little in common. He had to plan ahead for topics to discuss or there would be uncomfortable moments of silence. Of course, Agnes was eager to mention church events, who was getting married, who had a new baby, who was about to die. Generally, he let her do most of the talking, nodding, or murmuring an occasional comment. He always walked Agnes to her door, kissed her quickly on the cheek, and thanked her for the date.

Over the next couple of months when he had telephoned her to suggest an occasional outing, Agnes had explained that she already had a previous commitment or that she was feeling unwell. Taylor took the hint and found that he was immensely relieved when Agnes became unavailable.

Once a month *The Wallton Weekly* continued to post the announcement of the $500 reward offered by the bank for information leading to the murder of Jennifer Gower. For the first months after the incident, numerous people had come forward with what they thought was useful information. Unfortunately, all had been useless. Finally, as the year anniversary of the little girl's death drew near, Taylor had called and made an appointment to meet with George Allen.

He had not seen Barbara Hershey since his mother's party at the New Year, but she greeted him warmly and explained that "Mr. Allen is on the phone, but he'll be with you shortly."

As before when they had met, Taylor was impressed by Allen's office and the way the man was dressed. Although it was Wallton's usual hot August day, the banker wore a suit of light gray and a tie with red and blue stripes. Allen pointed Taylor to a seat in front of his desk and, as with their former meeting, turned one side of his face toward the window.

"Nothing of any merit come from the reward, Sheriff?"

"No. I got lots of calls. People said they saw all kinds of things. Think they may have just made up some of it. Nothing was of any help."

The two men sat for another few minutes, neither saying anything. As the silence grew, Taylor became uneasy. He wondered if he should add anything more or possibly just say he had to be somewhere. Finally, Allen broke the silence.

It won't hurt just to let the matter lie. Money will still be there if something does show up. Guess Dawson will still mention it in the paper from time to time.

"Fine with me," Taylor replied, "and I'm sure Mel will agree. As you say, something may turn up, but I doubt it. Been too long a time. Whoever did it is long gone."

"You're probably right, Sheriff. I guess not every crime can be solved."

As at their last meeting, Allen walked Taylor to the door of the office, thanked him for taking time to discuss the matter, and quickly returned to his desk when the phone began to ring.

"Busy day for you?" Taylor asked, lingering by Barbara's desk.

"Has been so far, and Mr. Allen has several appointments set up for this afternoon. I assume you're also busy.

"Seems like there's never a quiet moment, but nothing major. Just the normal round of complaints . . . usually about neighbors, a stray dog bothering someone, a loud noise that needs to be explained, but it does keep us busy. Well, I guess that's what we're paid to do."

"I'm sure it is," Hershey replied, adding nothing else to the conversation and leaving Taylor to make the next move.

"Well," he said again. "Guess I'd better get to it."

As he walked away from the bank, he shook his head. *Don't know why I find it so hard to talk with that woman, and she certainly doesn't make it any easier. Seems like she gets a kick out of leaving me hanging . . . trying to come up with something to say. Didn't have that problem with Agnes. She talked all the time, so I didn't have to say much . . .*

"Penny for your thoughts, Sheriff?"

Taylor stopped abruptly. He had not been paying attention to the other people on the sidewalk and was caught off guard. Looking up he saw Mel Dawson.

"Not worth a penny, Mel."

"Well, you were sure thinking hard about something. Must have been important."

"No, only about the reward money. Just spoke with Mr. Allen, and he's gonna keep offering it. Don't think it will do any good now as that death has been over a year with nothing happening. Still, he wants to do it. Imagine you will keep running it in the newspaper."

"Sure thing. Sometimes it makes filler when there's not much else to print of any interest."

"Well, good talking to you," Taylor said as the two reached a corner and turned in opposite directions.

Won't do any good but won't hurt either. Been too long now. Bank's money will still be there this time next year.

Taylor entered the office, stopped by Agnes' desk, and took a couple of phone messages from her.

———————•◆•———————

In terms of police work, the next months passed rather quietly for Taylor and his deputies. Oh, there had been a number of thefts, several assaults with minor injuries and a couple of knife fights with one man injured so badly that he had died from his wounds. Taylor had arrested his assailant, a cousin, and the man was duly tried, convicted and sentenced to prison for thirty-five years. Most of Wallton's crime problems had been of the usual minor nature and could be handled easily with some jail time or fines from Judge Maroney. He was feeling particularly content as he washed his hands at the kitchen sink after finishing his evening meal.

"Agnes Parsons is engaged, and the wedding is scheduled for this coming summer," Taylor's mother suddenly announced, an accusatory note in her voice.

"Good for her. I imagine we'll be invited to the wedding. Give her my congratulations if you run into her at church."

"Is that all you've got to say about it?" She followed him into the living room.

"What do you want me to say?" Taylor had turned the radio on, making sure that the volume was low.

"Aren't you the least bit interested that she's marrying another man? You squired her around quite a bit as I recall."

Taylor laughed at his mother's use of the word. "If you mean by 'squired' that I occasionally took her out, then I guess that's the right word. However, mother, I really had no interest in Agnes Parsons . . . romantic interest, if that's what you mean. You were the one interested in me becoming overly interested in her."

"Hmmph!" his mother snorted. "Well if you want to remain alone all of your life, that's fine with me. But Agnes would have made you a good wife, I can tell you. She's well-educated, responsible, pretty even."

"She's a nice woman and nice looking, I agree. Still, a little too churchy for my taste, mother." He laughed. "Now, instead of worrying about me getting married, you need to start thinking about a really nice wedding gift for Agnes . . . from the two of us."

———————◆◆◆———————

Taylor and his mother watched as Agnes Parsons, in a white gown and long veil carried a bouquet of crimson roses as she took her place beside the groom. Sandy-haired and only about an inch taller than Agnes, Timothy Robbe nervously placed a wedding band on his bride's finger. After a very brief kiss, the couple, followed by the bridesmaid and best man posed outside church with their respective parents for a photo before joining guests in the church basement at a receiving line.

Taylor dutifully kissed Agnes on the cheek, shook hands with her newly acquired husband and both sets of parents, and followed the wedding guests toward the refreshments. A wedding cake adorned with the traditional bride and groom was nestled on a plate surrounded by tiny pink flowers which Taylor did not recognize. He wondered if they had come from Doc Mason's garden. Various plates heaped with cookies and slices of apple and banana bread were placed near the cake on the long table. Plates of fudge and divinity were in evidence as well as a large bowl of mixed nuts. *Must have cost a pretty penny* Taylor thought as he knew almost any kind of nuts, even peanuts, were quite expensive. Taylor's mother, along with three other women handed out cups of punch as they encouraged everyone to take some of the "goodies."

Hot and uncomfortable in his suit, Taylor wished for his uniform. However, his mother had nearly had apoplexy when he had indicated that he didn't wish to wear a suit.

"You'll embarrass the life out of me," she had scolded. "You put on your good suit. As it is I just know that everyone will be looking at you and thinking that you lost out to that miner."

Glancing around the room, Taylor noticed several people who had been in school with him and assumed that they were friends of Agnes or her new husband. Since it appeared that all of Wallton's Protestants were at the ceremony, he had thought that George Allen might be at the reception but realized that the man was probably not a friend of the family, just a businessman who happened to own the only bank in town. Thinking of the banker brought back the few times they had met, the reward offered when Jennifer Gower was murdered, and the fact that he was no closer to solving the killing.

"Try not to look so glum," his mother admonished as she joined him. "Everyone will think you are sad at losing Agnes."

"Losing Agnes?" Taylor laughed heartily. "Mother, you can't lose something you never had and didn't want."

Then, late one evening as Taylor was relaxing at home, Deputy Drury called him. *Better meet me here at the office, Sheriff. Got a very upset father, and you need to hear this.*

Without waiting for any further explanation, Taylor immediately left the house and upon arriving at the office found Drury and Nathaniel Simmons waiting for him. Immediately Simmons rushed up to Taylor and yelled, "Sheriff, you know Dan Adams. You need to arrest Dan Adams now!"

"Whoa, Nat." Taylor knew Simmons from the hardware store which the man owned and where Taylor occasionally did some business. He was trying to recall if he knew Dan Adams. "Arrest him for what?"

"For what he did to my little girl. You've got to go and arrest him now!"

"Sit, Nat! Sit down and tell me the problem. You're not making any sense."

As Taylor shoved a chair toward the man, Simmons collapsed onto its seat, He started sobbing and rubbing his forehead, pushing a stray lock of sandy hair out of his eyes. Drury had poured a glass of water, and Taylor offered it to the distressed man who took a sip and handed it back, his sobs beginning to subside.

"Now, let us start from the beginning. Why should I arrest Dan Adams?

"He," Adams seemed unable to get words out. "He abused my little girl, my Nancy. He's an animal. You've got to arrest him."

For an instance Taylor thought he might not be hearing the man correctly. He glanced at Drury who merely nodded assent. It was obvious that Simmons had already explained his problem to the deputy.

"We'd better lock the door, Mr. Simmons. Don't want someone seeing me and the deputy come in here and them coming in to find out what's happening. They'll see that your lights are on." Leaning toward Simmons, Taylor asked him to explain as calmly as possible what he thought had happened to his daughter.

"Don't think, Sheriff. Know it for a fact. The Adams boy took Nancy into his attic and abused her. "She came home crying and told my wife. My wife's beside herself about it."

Now Taylor realized that Simmons was referring to a local boy although he couldn't seem to recall the youth. Taking a tablet from his desk, Taylor asked Simmons to go over the whole incident.

"Nancy went over to the Adams house," Simmons began. "She goes there sometimes to play with Mary Lou . . . has always done so. Mary Lou's the same age as Nancy. We've known the family for years, been good friends. Dan was always like a big brother to Nancy. Never thought anything about the three of them being together. Sort of like family they were."

Simmons stopped speaking, took a handkerchief from his pocket, and wiped his a tear from his eyes. Taylor could see it was an effort for the man to continue.

"Then tonight when my wife was getting Nancy ready for bed, she noticed that her panties were dirty. When she asked Nancy what she had been doing, Nancy told her that Dan had taken off her panties and dropped them on the floor when they were playing. My wife went into hysterics, Sheriff. I can tell you it was all I could do to keep her from going over to the Adams house with my gun. You've got to do something."

Taylor said he would look into the problem and finally got the distraught father somewhat calm. Looking at Drury, he told the deputy to take Mr. Simmons home and stay with him and his family until he could get to the home.

"Don't let them go over to the Adams' place. Under no circumstances let them do that," he instructed Drury. "I'm going to call Doc Mason, and we'll be there as soon as we can. You take the car. I'll get Doc to give me a ride."

Taylor could tell that his deputy was reluctant to take charge of the distraught father, but he helped Simmons to stand, then ushered him toward the office door and into the Taylor's auto. As they drove away, Taylor telephoned Mason who fortunately had not yet retired for the night, and quickly explained the problem, asking the doctor to stop by and give him a ride.

"Be there in a few minutes," Mason said. "Just got to put my shoes on and get locked up. Probably need to bring my kit."

Shortly, Mason and Taylor arrived at the Simmons home, and Mason ushered Mrs. Simmons and Nancy into a bedroom off of a small dining area. Taylor and Simmons, who had gotten his emotions somewhat under control, sat silently in the home's living room, its walls papered in small clumps of berries and pale blue stripes. After about fifteen minutes the doctor came back alone and joined Taylor and the father.

"Not rape," Mason explained, "but there might have been . . . some bit of probing . . . might have hurt the girl a little. I've got both your wife and daughter calmed down some, Mrs. Simmons. Gave them something . . . something mild . . . to help them get some sleep. That's the best thing for now . . . will help the most right now." He looked toward Taylor. "You want me to stay?"

"No, Doc. Thanks for coming so hurriedly. Deputy Drury is waiting outside and can drive me back to the office later on."

As Mason walked out, Taylor turned to Simmons. "I need some more information, Nat."

"Okay," Simmons responded, his head down. "What else is there for me to tell you?"

"First, how old is Nancy, and do you know how old the Adams boy is?"

"Nancy's nine, be ten in two months. Don't know how old that boy is. Probably around fifteen or sixteen. Know he's in high school. Lot older than my little girl. Can't believe he'd do a thing like this." Simmons voice caught, and Taylor was afraid he was going to start weeping again.

"Think, Nat," Taylor said abruptly. "Has Nancy always gone over to the Adams house? Has the boy ever come over here?"

"Don't think so. The little Adams girl, Sheila, comes over. She and Nancy are good friends, play together, in the same class at school . . . Simmons grabbed Taylor's arm. "School? Hadn't thought about that. How's Nancy gonna go to school? Everyone will know about this, point her out . . . Wife says she's ruined, Sheriff. No one will want their kids around her . . ."

Although he tried to tell Simmons that his last comments were not true, Taylor knew they were. Even if the little girl was unaware that something considered bad had happened to her, from this day on Nancy would always be "ruined" in the eyes of the town. He would try to keep the incident quiet. Musso would not tell anyone, and Mason was always the "soul of discretion." Still, he would have to investigate Simmon's charge. Even if there were no arrest, as Simmons wished, news would leak out. He had seen lights go on in a neighboring home as he and Mason had arrived. The sheriff going out late at night always brought questions and speculation.

"I'll talk to the Adams boy tomorrow morning, Mr. Simmons. Not tonight. Better not to get the whole neighborhood stirred up tonight. Need to keep this as quiet as we can for the time being. It won't help your little girl to have this the latest topic of gossip."

Taylor left the father sitting dejectedly in his now quiet living room, joined Drury, and told the deputy to drive away before any neighbors came outside.

Shortly after seven the next morning Taylor drove to the Adams home, a two-story painted light gray with a wide wrap-around porch. He knew it would be breakfast time and wished to talk with the Adams boy before he left for school.

"Morning, Sheriff," Paul Adams said, a puzzled expression on his face. "You're out awful early, aren't you? Something wrong at the store?"

No, store's fine." Adams was referring to Wallton's drug store which he owned. A pharmacist himself, Adams provided the prescription medicine for the town, most of which Doc Mason prescribed. In addition to himself, Adams had working for him a young man who was training to be a pharmacist and a woman about forty-five years old, a window who sold the store's other goods and took care of the soda fountain.

"Mr. Adams," Taylor said formally, although he had known the man for many years. "This is not a social call. I need to speak with you and with your son. Is he still at home?"

"Well, yeah, he's having breakfast. Come on in." Adams appeared confused but led Taylor into the family's kitchen.

Seated at the kitchen table were Mrs. Adams, a baby girl in a high chair, a young girl who Taylor assumed was the friend of Nancy Simmons, and a boy who stood up as the two men entered.

Not a boy, Taylor thought as the boy stood up and he noted Dan Adams' size. *About five foot eight and beefy. Must weigh nearly 160 pounds.*

"What's wrong, Paul?" Mrs. Adams looked at her husband.

"Nothing, Mary. Nothing. Sheriff just wants to talk with me and Dan. You and the girls finish your breakfast." He motioned to his son.

"Dad, I've got to finish dressing. I'll be late for school."

"You've got time. Come on, now." The three walked out of the kitchen and into a large comfortable living room. Taylor noted that like him, Adams had a piano and a radio. The two men settled into dark leather chairs, but the boy remained standing.

"Well," Adams said. "What's the problem? Dan and those two cronies he hangs out with up to some mischief?"

There was no easy way to explain his visit. Looking directly at Adams, he said quietly, "Mr. Simmons has accused Dan of . . ." Taylor was looking for the right words . . . "inappropriately fondling his little daughter."

Actually Simmons implied it was more than fondling, but I want to see how the boy will react. Couldn't think of any other way to put it. Not an easy accusation to make . . . Don't want to make it into something it isn't, especially until I get more information . . . much more information.

"What? What?" Adams looked at Taylor and then at his son. "Are you saying Dan and the little girl . . ." The father gasped for words and then turned to his son.

"Did you hear? Do you hear what the sheriff is saying? Do you know what he's saying, Dan?"

"I didn't do nothin! I didn't do nothin!" Dan exclaimed loudly, and Taylor could see a hint of fear on the boy's face.

"Calm down! Lower your voice! Do you hear me!" Turning to Taylor, Adams said. "There's got to be some mistake . . . an awful mistake. You can't think my boy would do something like that?"

"Mr. Adams," Taylor once again addressed the man formally. "The charge had been made, and I have to look into it. You understand. I have to investigate the matter."

"You're gonna take my son to your office . . . to jail? You're arresting him? Is that what you're saying? You're putting him in jail?" Adam's voice rose higher. "You're taking Simmons' word as if it is truth?"

"Please calm down, Mr. Adams. I'm not taking Dan to jail. I have told you the accusation, and I just need to ask Dan a few questions. Have to ask some questions." Taylor didn't wish the meeting to get more out of hand than it already was and spoke calmly, looking at the boy.

"Dan, you understand that I'm just trying to clear up the situation . . . just doing my job?"

"I didn't do nothing," the boy cried again. "That man is lying to you." He turned to his father, and Taylor could see the fear in his eyes. "He's lying, dad. He's lying. Why's he lying?"

"Let the sheriff ask his questions," Adams barked. "We need to get this . . . mistake cleared up."

Taylor could feel the tension in the room as he asked, "Dan, was Nancy Simmons over here yesterday?"

"Yeh, I think so." The boy answered.

"Was she, or wasn't she?" his father interrupted harshly.

"Yeh, she was."

The boy hung his head, and Taylor knew then that something had happened, something inappropriate as Nancy's father had charged. How inappropriate Taylor would try to discern while trying to be as circumspect as possible. He could see the beginning of tears on the boy's face and the growing anger on the father's face. In fact, he thought Simmons might strike his son.

"Did Nancy . . . disrobe?" Taylor asked quietly.

"Dad, I didn't do nothin! Nothin! Nancy is lying. I didn't do nothin." Dan cried loudly, cringing as he looked at his father and avoided answering Taylor's question

Taylor knew then that something had happened in the attic and also knew that Adams had come to the same conclusion. He could see the anger grow in Adam's face and needed to make certain that the father didn't attack his son. He also didn't wish the rest of the family to hear the noise and suddenly appear in the room. Time enough later for Simmons to tell his wife what had transpired.

"I would suggest," Taylor began quietly, "that you stay home from school today, Dan. Have your mom call and say you're sick. I would also suggest that you don't contact your friends and tell them what has happened. Best thing right now is to keep this matter quiet, until I can look into it more. You understand wha I'm saying?"

Both the shaken son and his father nodded assent, and then Adams asked, "What's going to happen now, Sheriff? Will the whole town hear of this? What's that gonna do to my business . . . to my wife and little girl? They won't be able to hold their heads up. You know how this town is. We'll be the talk of the town."

Taylor knew what the pharmacist said was true. He had urged Nancy's father to say nothing. He knew that Deputy Musso and Doc Mason would say nothing. Still, neighbors on both sides of the street had seen his car and knew something was amiss. He also felt that Simmons would not let the matter drop. He would need to speak again with both Nancy Simmons and Dan Adams. Once more, neighbors would see his auto at the two homes.

"What about my business?" Adams echoed his earlier question. "My business will be ruined. I'll have to leave . . . sell my house . . ."

Taylor hoped this would not be the case. Adam's business was the only pharmacy in town and was badly needed. Adams was the only pharmacist; his apprentice was not licensed to dispense medications except under the supervision of Adams.

"Don't jump the gun, Paul." It was the first time Taylor had addressed the man less formally. "Give me some time to see what I can do, how this is all gonna shake out. I will have to do some more investigating. You understand that? It's my job, and I need to make sure I do it . . . right . . . as right as I can for both Simmons' daughter and your son."

Taylor looked at Dan Adams who stayed hunched over and didn't meet Taylor's eyes. His father walked Taylor to the door and quietly closed it behind him. Already neighbors were up and out with one asking, "Trouble, Sheriff?"

"Nothin much. Just need to get some information about some medicine . . . did get a free cup of coffee from Mrs. Adams."

Instead of going to the office, Taylor drove a few miles outside of Wallton and parked, slumping tiredly against the seat as he thought about the whole situation. He would try to keep the problem quiet, but he knew this would be impossible. Either the little girl would talk to her little friends, or the mother would feel the need to tell a relative or close friend. He also felt that Simmons was not going to let the matter drop even though it would bring immense problems for both his and the Adams family. It would be the talk of the town for months, just like the Jennifer Gower murder.

There had been another such incident a few years back, and Taylor knew it was due to boys and sex – their need to know about it, to have questions answered, to experiment. He could recall that it had been frequently the topic of conversation when he and his male classmates gathered in the locker room to change clothing before gym class.

Growing up on the ranch, Taylor knew about sex between animals; it was the reason calves got born. Although he had never asked, and it certainly had never been discussed with him by his father, as a boy he had just assumed it must be similar between people. During his sophomore year in high school he had his first sexual rendezvous, two actually, with a neighbor girl who was a senior. A couple of year after he became a deputy, he had entered into a year-long liaison with a married woman from the next county but had broken it off, fearing that someone would find out. He was pretty certain that, like most teenage boys, Dan Adams' curiosity had led to the incident with the little Simmons girl.

Then suddenly, a new thought entered his mind, and he sat up straighter. *Could Dan Adams be the person who killed Jennifer? Could he? Could it have been the result of an incident with Jennifer similar to the one now facing the Adams' boy? Only she resisted and that incident had turned fatal.*

That death was almost two years ago so he'd have been around fourteen or so. He's a big boy, looks strong. Certainly could have strangled that little girl. He would have been older than the Gower boys . . . Still he lived not far from the Gower home . . . would have been around the area walking or biking from school. The boys would have known him, and Jennifer would have seen him around . . .

"No!" Taylor said loudly. "No way!" Still the thought was there . . . nagging . . . tormenting. It was a possibility. He couldn't get the idea out of his mind. It would explain Jennifer Gower's death and his belief that the murderer was someone local. He started the car and drove slowly back into Wallton.

———◆———

As Taylor had known the incident, "the Adams - Simmons problem" as it was called, gradually became known and circulated around the town.

"The news is out, Sheriff," Alma said shortly after eight o'clock one morning. "Everyone's talking. I even get calls here at work."

"I know, Alma. Hard to keep something like that quiet."

"Not because of me," Alma protested. "I didn't say anything. You asked me to keep it quiet. I did."

"It's not you, Alma. I asked both parties not to talk to anyone, and they said they didn't intend to, but . . ."

Taylor knew how the incident became known around the community. First, he had talked again with both Simmons and Adams. Hoping to avoid the curiosity of Simmons' neighbors, he had gone to the hardware store owned by the man and spoke quietly with him. He had explained that there was little he could do about the incident. Simmons had made the complaint; Adams' son had denied that anything had happened. It became a case of "she says," and "he denies."

"Well, they sure got the boy out of town in a hurry. Doesn't that tell you something, Sheriff? Doesn't that tell you that he was guilty?" Simmons had barked as Taylor kept him informed about the investigation.

While he didn't say so, Taylor felt that something had happened in the Adams attic, but he doubted that the truth would ever come out. Within a week of his second visit to speak with Dan Adam's father, his son had been on a train out of Wallton. The explanation given to those who asked about the boy's absence was that Mr. Adams' father back in Indiana had been injured in an accident, and the boy was needed to help out on the family farm. Adams couldn't leave the town without a pharmacy, so the son had to take his place in Indiana.

Apparently, Mrs. Simmons had felt the need to tell someone. She had confided to a close friend, who had promised not to tell anyone. However, she also had a close friend, who also promised not to tell, who then told a close friend, and the story soon spread like wildfire. Neighbors took sides. The boy did it. The boy didn't do anything. The other little girls at school whispered behind Nancy's back, sending her home crying many afternoons. Both Mrs. Adams and Mrs. Simmons could see people whispering to each other when they left home to shop. The situation was intolerable. Within a few weeks the two husbands became bachelors as the remainder of their families either took the train or drove away from Wallton to "visit relatives."

For Taylor, however, the thought that Dan Adams could have been the individual who killed Jennifer Gower interfered with his life. Sometimes it crept into his thoughts while he had an idle moment in the office; often at night it prevented him from drifting to sleep. Finally, he decided to visit Mason.

Once again he waited in the gathering dusk outside the doctor's home. A heavy late summer shower had dampened the festivities of the Labor Day weekend but had been welcomed by most as the summer had been "a scorcher." Now, at only the middle of September, trees already were beginning to shed a few leaves, and the evening air felt brisk enough that Taylor considered rolling up the car window. He could see no persons outside their homes and assumed that families were now busy enjoying a late evening meal or children ready for bed.

It was nearly two hours before the doctor's car lights pierced the darkness. Taylor waited until the man approached his yard before calling to him.

"Am I the only friend you got that you can visit late at night?" Mason asked as Taylor shut his car door.

Taylor laughed. "No one as interesting as you, Doc. You too tired or do you have a few minutes to talk?"

"Well, I'm tired, as always. But come on in. I just hope this is a social call and not some kind of nasty business."

The two men walked into the house, and Taylor waited while Mason made a pot of coffee and put together a sparse meal. Neither had spoken more than a few words, and Taylor thought about how he would approach the reason he had been sitting once again outside the physician's home.

"Doc," he began softly after taking another sip of the coffee Mason had given him. "I know you're gonna think I should put the Gower girl's death to rest. I know I should. It's past and done with, but I just can't seem to let it go. It just keeps bothering me from time to time. Can't solve it. Can't let it go. You understand?"

Mason put his napkin on top of his plate and pushed it away. Taking another sip of his coffee, he nodded his head.

"Know what you're saying. Get the same problem sometimes. Have a patient who's very ill, most likely dying. Don't want to just come out and say that, so I beat around the bush. Nothin' I can do to make the outcome different, but it preys on my mind."

Taylor waited a moment, and then just blurted out, "Do you think the Adams boy could have killed that little girl?"

Mason knew to whom Taylor was referring and waited a moment before replying, looking long and hard at the sheriff. "Possibly. You must think so or you wouldn't be asking me."

"Well, I've thought and thought about it. Keeps just running through my mind at odd times. He was big enough, even two years ago. She probably knew him or had seen him. Even if she yelled, who'd have heard her or paid any attention? Kids yell all the time when they play. You know that."

"Think he tried to play with her like he did the Simmons girl? She fought, made a stir, and he killed her trying to keep her quiet?"

"Don't know." Taylor rubbed his forehead. "Just don't know, and it's only an idea. Hate to think it could be true. Even if it is, can't do anything about it now. Boy is gone, and it's only something that keeps bothering me. Don't have anything that actually points to Dan." It was the first time Taylor had used the boy's name.

Mason got up and refilled their coffee cups, sinking heavily back onto his chair. The two sat, saying nothing, the silence settling around them. Finally Taylor broke the silence.

"Did a little looking at other kids dying," Taylor began quietly. "Looked through months of old newspapers. Remember, I asked you about one of the kids?"

"I recall," Mason replied. "Not a girl; young boy. Died from a head injury. You asked me about that almost a year ago. Don't see how the two could be connected."

"Guess they really aren't, Doc, but there was another boy died from an accident a few years before that one. Just seems odd. Not saying the Adams boy had anything to do with those two, but three kids dead in this little town . . . keeps bothering me."

The two sat silently for several minutes, each in their own thoughts. Finally, Mason said, "Tell you what. Let it go for now." He got up and opened a cabinet. "Neighbor lady, Mrs. Elliott, very nice lady, brought me a cherry pie. Forgot I had it. Let me cut us a piece."

The doctor got the pie, cut each a large slice and added some more coffee to their cups. The pie was sweet and juicy, and the two men sat silently for a few minutes. Then Mason broke the silence.

"You know I don't repeat what you tell me or what happens with patients in my office. Still," he hesitated for a moment, "your mother stopped by a couple of weeks ago. Nothin' wrong. Just a regular checkup." Mason said hurriedly. Didn't know if she mentioned it to you."

"No, she certainly didn't!" Taylor exclaimed.

"Well, now just you don't go and tell her I told tales out of school. She's fine . . . just fine . . . but like me, she's not getting any younger. Just thought you should know. Keep an eye on her."

"I'll be sure to do that, and I won't let her know I know anything," Taylor said, "but I am a bit worried. I've noticed that she's slowed down some."

After taking a final sip of his coffee, Taylor helped Mason clear the table, bid the man goodnight and walked to his car. He hesitated for a minute before starting the engine, mulling over Mason's last few words. *Now how am I going to be able to ask Mom how she feels without her becoming suspicious?*

———————◆•◆•◆———————

"Two people say they need to see you, Sheriff," Alma said late on a Friday afternoon near the end of September. She stood in the doorway to his office, hands on her hips. "From outside town, I think. Don't usually get people dropping by just to see you this late on a Friday afternoon. Asked if I could help them, but they want to see you. So there must be some kind of bad trouble. Wouldn't tell me what it's about."

"Show them in, Alma," Taylor replied. He stood up, moved around his desk and held the door for the couple to enter. The man, a little stooped, wore bib overalls and a denim jacket over what appeared to be a plaid flannel shirt. Following behind was a tiny woman dressed in a short black coat and clutching tightly at a large purse. Both had lank brown hair and light hazel eyes, and to Taylor, the woman appeared to be considerably younger than the man.

"You're from a ways out beyond the Catholic cemetery, aren't you?" Taylor couldn't remember their names but recalled seeing them occasionally, probably when they came into Wallton to do some shopping.

"Clem Johnson, Sheriff." The man extended his hand to Taylor. "And this is my wife, Ruthie." The woman merely nodded, smiled slightly and then looked down at the floor.

"Good to meet both of you. Let me get a couple of chairs, and then you can tell me what brings you to Wallton."

Taylor hastily carried the chairs into his office and, after seating the two, made sure his door was firmly shut. Alma didn't need to hear the conversation. She'd know soon enough if something was amiss.

"Now, what's the problem"

"Our boy's gone missing," the woman exclaimed immediately.

"Now, Ruthie," Clem Johnson interrupted, patting her hand. "We don't know that for sure."

"Well he ain't come home, has he?" Ruthie Johnson stated bluntly as she fought to keep back tears.

"Why don't you tell me exactly what has happened," Taylor began. "Just take your time, and we'll try and sort everything out. How old is the boy?"

"Our boy, Robert – we call him Bobby is eleven – goes to school in town." Johnson paused for a minute and then continued. "We live just south of town about five miles . . . You know my place, Sheriff?"

"Yes, I do," Taylor replied. Now he remembered Johnson. The man worked at a coal mine but had a house on a few acres of scrub land close to Wallton.

"Well, since my boy has to walk to school . . . I don't let him take one of the horses . . . he stays in town at a friend's house Monday through Wednesday nights – the Hansons. They're some kind of distant relative of my wife." Johnson paused and looked at his wife who continued staring at the floor. "Then he's home on Thursday and Friday evenings to help with chores . . . help feed the chickens and milk the cow, bring in water and wood . . . Also his being home those nights makes his momma not feel so alone, just her and our other two younger kids."

"You're gone all the other nights?"

"Yep. I leave at the crack of dawn on Monday for the mine and don't usually get home until really late on a Friday, sometimes on Saturday, as it's nearly an eight-mile walk both ways. Can't complain about the schedule as I do have a job . . . luckier than some folks. Reason I'm here this evening early is my missus got word to the mine that Bobby hadn't come home. The superintendent let me go early and even gave me a ride home."

"Somethin's happened to my boy, Sheriff." The mother interrupted again, I just know it. Somethin' bad. School's only been going for three weeks, and he's gone."

"Have you spoken to Bobby's friend, Mr. Johnson? Maybe he has an explanation."

"Went there before we came here, Sheriff. That boy, Eugene Hanson's his name, said he and Bobby talked after school, played marbles for a few minutes. Then Bobby left and Eugene went on home. That's the last time he saw Bobby. Don't think he's lying . . . do you?"

"I doubt it, Mr. Johnson, but I will certainly speak with the boy. Now, let me ask both of you a few more questions." Turning to the mother, Taylor asked, "Haven't had any problems with Bobby, Mrs. Johnson. No angry words . . . anything like that?"

"Nuthin', Sheriff. Nuthin' at all. Bobby comes home, has a bite to eat as he's always hungry, and goes about his chores. He knows what has to be done around the place . . . doesn't complain much . . . just does what he has to do. What am I gonna do if he doesn't come home?" Tears began to trickle down Ruthie Johnson's cheeks, but she made no sound.

"No problems between you and Bobby, Mr. Johnson?" Taylor shifted his questioning to the father. "Sometimes boys and their fathers don't always see eye to eye."

Taylor could remember a few times when he and his father had words, usually over something Taylor had forgotten to do and what he had considered unimportant. His father had never physically abused him; just the tone of his father's voice when he was angry or disappointed with his son made Taylor do what was necessary. He felt that if there had been an argument, particularly a physical one, between Johnson and his son that the boy might have stayed away because he was fearful or maybe just plain angry.

"Well, yeh. We do get into it sometimes, if that's what you're asking. But I don't beat Bobby. You can ask the missus. We both just holler at him or the other kids when they need it. We never hurt the boy or his kin."

"You have other children, Mrs. Johnson?"

"Oh, yes, I do. We lost a girl to measles back a few years ago." She peered at her husband and then added. "Now I have left the two boys four and six and Bobby . . . just turned eleven two months ago."

"Where are your other children, Mrs. Johnson?"

"Why at home, Sheriff. We couldn't drag them all the way in here. They're too little." Ruthie Johnson looked anxiously at her husband. "They're fine being left alone, Clem. Aren't they?"

"They'll be fine. Just fine. We be goin' home soon." Johnson patted his wife's hand.

"Do you have a picture of Bobby, Mrs. Johnson? If not, can you tell me a little bit about him? What he looks like?"

"Well, he's got real blonde hair but dark brown eyes. He's quite a bit smaller than some boys his age, but he'll grow into that in a few years. I don't have a picture of him. We've been meaning to do that . . . get all three of the boys . . . but . . ." Ruthie's words died, and she looked anxiously at her husband before saying quietly, "You know, money's tight these days."

"It certainly is, Mrs. Johnson." Taylor was quick to agree with her. He didn't wish to have any kind of argument begin between the couple, and he felt that Johnson might take his wife's last comment as condemnation on his ability to provide an adequate income for his family.

"No place around town that you think the boy might have stopped off yesterday, Mr. Johnson? Other than the Hansons? Another friend? A store, perhaps? Boys like to look at all kinds of things. Maybe the dime store, the hardware store . . . or the drug store for a soda or a lime phosphate?"

"Not Bobby. He ain't never got no money for a soda. He always comes straight home, and now it's two days he's gone. He knows his mother needs him. He and his mother are very close . . . tied at the apron strings, as we used to say."

"Well, let me get things moving." Taylor went to the door, opened it and called to Alma. "Know it's getting late, Alma, but before you leave, could you locate Deputy Warren and ask him to stop by before he heads for home. Need to see him before he goes off shift."

Turning to the Johnsons, he asked, "How're you folks getting home?"

"Oh, we'll just walk. Won't take us too long," Johnson replied.

"Let me give you and your wife a ride. You don't want to be away from the rest of your children too long. I'll be in touch with you after we take a look around town. Sure we'll find Bobby somewhere." Taylor smiled at Mrs. Johnson, hoping his words would reassure her.

Ushering the two parents to his car, Taylor put Mrs. Johnson in the back seat and drove south. It now was after five o'clock, and although the sun lingered fairly high in the western sky, a few dark clouds were gathering on the horizon, a hint that rain might not be too far off. He hoped that if it did rain, it would be just a quick shower, and the boy would be able to find some shelter.

———◆———

Later that evening, as he drove back into Wallton, Taylor thought about the two parents and their missing child. Even thought it was nearing dusk and several windows already showed lights, he would have to go up to the Hanson home immediately and speak with Eugene Hanson. He was fairly certain that the Hanson boy could provide little more information than that given by the Johnsons. Still he hoped Eugene might remember some little thing that would be of help, something he might have forgotten or something he hadn't thought he should tell the parents in case it would get the missing boy in trouble.

Then his thoughts turned to the Johnson boy. Why had Bobby Johnson not gone home? Where was he? Did he have other friends with whom he could stay, or was the Hanson home the only place of refuge? If, as the Johnsons had indicated, the boy was not a discipline problem and had always done what was expected of him, what caused this sudden change in his behavior?

He's probably just at some other kid's house, and time has got away from him . . . kids playing and all that. I hope Max Warren is waiting for me when I get back to the office so we can track the kid down. However, his thoughts did not comfort him. Somehow he knew something was very wrong. He just didn't know what.

It was nearly dusk as Taylor drove up to the Hanson home, but he could see a boy and a dog in the front yard.

"Nice dog you got there," he said as he neared the two. "I'm Sheriff Taylor, by the way. Are you Arnold?"

"I know you," the boy replied. "I'm Gene, but I didn't do nothing."

"Oh, I'm not here about you doing anything. I just wanted to know if you saw Bobby Johnson yesterday?"

"Sure. He was here. We came home after we got out of school, played some marbles for a while. Then he had to go home. You want to talk to my mother?"

"That would be fine," Taylor responded as he followed the boy and his dog, a large Collie, toward the house. The Taylor home, a large white-painted clapboard, was situated about the middle of a neatly kept small lot. Taylor seemed to remember that the boy's father worked at J. C. Penney – possibly as the manager of the store.

"Mom," Gene Hanson called loudly. "The sheriff's here."

Within a minute Mrs. Hanson appeared, wiping her hands on a dishcloth and pushing a lock of hair out of her eyes. She apparently had been baking something for their supper as there was flour on her apron, and a wisp of it had settled on her nose.

"What's wrong?" she cried immediately upon seeing the two. "What's happened? Has something happened to my husband? Has Eugene done something wrong?" Taylor noted that his mother called the boy by his full name although the boy referred to himself as Gene.

Why is it whenever people see me, they always immediately ask if something's wrong? They always assume that I'm bringing bad news, and I guess most times I am. Even when I go to see Doc Mason, it's usually with bad news. Guess I don't just make friendly calls . . .

"Nothing's wrong, ma'am. Your husband's fine . . . still at work, I assume, and Gene's done nothing wrong." Taylor quickly assured the woman and could see the fear fade from her eyes. "I just need to ask you a little bit about the Johnson boy – Bobby. I understand that he stays with you folks a couple of nights each week during school."

"Yes, that's right." She breathed a sigh of relief. "You scared me. I thought something had happened to my husband or that Eugene had got in some kind of trouble." She smiled and swiped at the flour on her nose.

"I didn't mean to yell like that. Yes," to answer your question, "Bobby Johnson stays here three nights a week. It's really no trouble. Arnie has bunk beds in his room, and Bobby is nice and polite, and we are distant relatives . . . quite distant, I think." She realized that she had been babbling and surprised, but you know how boys are? They seem to find ways . . ."

"No, No. He's caused no trouble," Taylor interrupted. "It's just that

Bobby didn't come home last night or hasn't come this evening, and his folks are getting worried."

"Eugene, when did he leave?" Mrs. Hanson demanded, turning to look at her son.

"About a half hour after school yesterday, mom. The way he always does on Thursdays. We only played a couple of games of marbles, and then he said he had to go. We didn't fight or nothin' . . . just played marbles."

"Was he at school today, Gene?" Taylor asked.

He knew it was too late in the evening to find anyone still at the school. Monday, he would have to locate the boy's teacher and check with her to see if there had been any kind of problem.

"No, but I just thought he might be sick or maybe one of his brothers were. He has to help his mom, you know?"

"You don't think something bad has happened, do you, Sheriff?" Mrs. Hanson peered anxiously at Taylor. "He's just a little boy, and he has a long way to walk to get home. Could he have fallen into an arroya or something?"

"We're certainly going to look at every possibility, Mrs. Hanson. You'll be among the first to know what we find, and . . . by the way, I'd appreciate it if you wouldn't say anything about this right now. You, too, Gene."

"Of course, of course. I'll only mention it to my husband, and Arnie will keep quiet also."

Taylor thanked the two and walked out to his car. He knew that probably Mrs. Hanson would keep the incident quiet but Eugene . . . that was another story. He knew kids. If he were still a kid, Taylor was certain that he, too, would begin to spread the word about the missing Bobby Johnson.

Returning to the office, Taylor found Deputy Max Warren waiting outside. While all of the employees had keys, the place was kept open daily only during the week and on Saturday and Sunday if there were a need. Unlocking the door, Taylor turned on the light and motioned Warren to enter.

"Got a missing boy, Max," Taylor began as the deputy followed him. "I've spoken with the parents who reported that the boy, Bobby Johnson about eleven years old, has not been home tonight . . . well, it'll be two nights now. Wondered if you might have seen a kid wandering around this late in the evening?"

"No, Sheriff, but I might not have paid any attention if I had," Warren replied. "See a lot of kids out and about all the time. Don't notice unless they're into some kind of trouble." Warren rubbed his head thoughtfully as if trying to recall anything out of the ordinary and then asked, "Anything especially unusual about this kid?"

"Not really . . . blonde, brown eyes . . . just a kid. Oh, yes, his mother said that he was small for his size. Might be something. Might not. At any rate, you have at least two more hours on your shift. Keep an eye out particularly in alleys. Seems like kids always play in alleys. I'll get the word to the other guys tomorrow, but right now I'll drive around the lower part of town myself."

Taylor roamed slowly up and down each street and alley, hoping to see in the auto's lights some sign of the Johnson boy. By now it was dark, and a slight mist began to fall. He felt that if the boy still had been outside walking, he would have tried to find some shelter. There were many places someone could hide – sheds, garages with doors left open, piles of wood or lumber, even under a vehicle. It was pointless to continue the search that night. He and his men would begin early the next morning, and by then, he knew, they would have additional help as people began to learn of the missing child.

"You're so late," his mother scolded as he walked in the door. "I've tried to keep your supper warm, but I know the meat is all dried out by now."

"Sorry, mom. It'll be fine. Just had some last minute things come up and couldn't get away. Supper will be just fine. I hope you already ate instead of waiting for me."

Taylor was surprised that his mother did not ask any questions about his delay in getting home and realized that news of the missing boy had not reached her yet. Perhaps Mrs. Hanson and her son had followed his advice and not mentioned the problem, at least for this evening. By tomorrow he knew the whole town would know.

—————◆◆◆—————

At six O'clock Saturday morning Taylor was at the Johnsons' place south of town, a tiny house of rough, unpainted boards with a tar-paper roof. Nearby was a lean-to containing two horses, and a privy was situated a little further away. Scratching at the remains of the corn from what had been their evening supper, a few chickens stirred up the dust. He knew that Clem Johnson would already have left to walk to his job at the coal mine as the miners worked six days a week and sometimes on Sunday, especially in the colder months when the demand for coal was heaviest. However, he wished to find out if perhaps Bobby had returned to his home sometime during the night hours. He had not.

Taylor found Mrs. Johnson still a bit weepy as she invited him into the house. As he sat drinking a cup of coffee, he looked around the small room. Two worn leather chairs with a table between them made up what he thought was the parlor area, the rest of the room containing a table and six chairs with a sink of sorts and some dilapidated cabinets clutching one wall. He knew all water used in the home had to be brought from a well and wondered if the two young boys staring at him could be of any help to heir mother.

"I've already got all my men out looking for Bobby, Mrs. Johnson. The Hansons said he left their place shortly after school Wednesday, and they assumed he was going home. We're also checking out any place he might hide . . . also the arroyas between here and town, in case he might have stumbled into one and couldn't climb out."

"Can't imagine he'd do that," Ruthie Johnson responded. "He's not given to going across country. He'd have just stayed on the road like he always does."

Taylor thought the woman was probably right. Walking off the road would have been laborious, and Bobby also would know that he might stumble over a rattlesnake. The kid had to be in town.

The phone was ringing as Taylor entered the office an hour later, and he knew the news was out. He called Alma, explained the problem and asked if she could come in to work. He didn't have time to answer the dozens of phone calls from concerned or just plain nosy citizens. Deputies would be coming back in all morning to report on what they had or hadn't found. He hoped, desperately hoped, that one of the men would have located Bobby. He also knew that a fairly large number of Wallton's residents would be out hunting for the boy.

Yet by late afternoon the results of the canvass proved fruitless. People – men, women, children – had roamed the town looking in any place a boy might hide. Bobby Johnson could not be found. Taylor would have to make another trip out to the Johnson's place to give the couple the bad news.

"You've hardly eaten anything," his mother scolded as she cleaned up the evening mea she had kept for him in the warming oven. "You can't find the boy if he's not to be found."

"I know, mother. I know." Taylor said despondently. "I'm just not hungry tonight."

"You'll find him. I know you will." She stopped talking and then asked, "Could he have left town? Could he have caught one of the trains and left town?"

"We thought of that," Taylor replied. "We've asked that any boxcars that have gone through Wallton in the past two days be checked in case he did that. So far, several tramps were aboard but no boy."

"What about the creek? I hear the water's been a little high. Maybe he decided to go for a wade to cool off, although it hasn't been that hot now that summer's gone . . . not like it was in July and August."

The creek! Hadn't really thought of that but mother's right. Maybe Bobby just thought it would be fun to wade around for a bit. Water has been a bit high but not much. Course he might have slipped, hit his head . . . or broken a leg and couldn't get out. Still, you'd think he would have heard any people out searching for him calling his name as they walked over the bridge. Wonder if anyone went into the creek.

"Hadn't really thought about the creek, mother. Maybe my men went down near the water, but I don't know that for sure. I'll get a couple of deputies and go there right now. Won't be able to see much as it's already dark, but Bobby could hear us if we yell. If he's not too bad hurt, he could yell back."

Taylor got Musso, Drury, and Sam Edson and headed down to the creek. The three of them waded into the water which was nearly two feet deep and cold. Calling the boy's name, they moved both up and down the stream and waited expectantly, but no replay came. Each man had a flashlight and scanned the bank; however, the darkness sucked up the light.

"No point in going farther," Drury said as both he and Edson stopped walking. "Not gonna find anything now. Can't see anything more than a couple of feet in front of us."

Taylor knew the deputy was right. He also knew that if the boy were in the creek and hurt, he would have cried out when he heard the men. Of course, if he were unconscious . . . Taylor didn't wish to contemplate that idea further.

"You're right. Let's get out of this water. We'll come back at daylight . . . go further down . . . maybe find him then."

Taylor knew that was just an idle comment. They would come back and search in the morning, but he was certain that Bobby Johnson was not in the creek.

———◆◆◆———

Just after daylight on Sunday, Taylor and the three deputies who also had helped search the previous night were once again picking their way along the creek, careful not to fall on the slippery rocks. A few of the bushes along the banks had already lost most of their summer leaves, and the morning air was brisk. Like the previous evening, the men called out the boy's name as they plodded further downstream. Nothing reached their ears except an occasional gurgle as water washed over a few rocks.

"Might as well go," Taylor said after two hours. "We're not gonna find anything here. He's not down here. We'll try another search of the town."

The canvass would be useless. Even though both Taylor and his deputies prowled the streets and alleys until dark on Sunday, probing into many small spaces where someone might be concealed, they found nothing.

On Monday morning, Taylor went to the Wallton grade school, a building of light tan bricks constructed just over three years previously. Talking in the hall with Miss Naomi Grier, Bobby's fifth grade teacher, he asked about the boy's attendance and school work.

"He's a good student, Sheriff," Grier responded as she pushed a stray bit of gray hair back from eyes nearly the same color. Taylor recalled that Miss Grier had been his fifth-grade teacher and had looked the same way all those years ago as she did now – pale skin, gray hair cut short, and a dress with long sleeves even when the weather became hot late in May .

"Bobby might have to miss a day of school, usually on a Friday," Grier added. "When school began three weeks ago, his father sent me a note, badly written as I recall, explaining that his son might have to be away from class sometimes to help out the mother. Bobby didn't show up last Friday, and I just assumed he was at home."

Taylor asked Grier if the boy was prone to getting in fights with other boys his age or older. Again the teacher indicated that if he had been in a fight, she was not aware of it. She also stated that she had not seen any cuts or bruises on him "except for what you would expect to see on an active boy who is playing various games."

Then Taylor checked with several individuals who worked around the train station and those who shunted trains through Wallton and on to northern or southern destinations. No one recalled seeing any boys near the depot or tracks during the past three or four days. If Bobby had "jumped" a train, no one had seen him do so.

Taylor knew he had exhausted every source that might lead to the boy's disappearance. He would need to tell Levi Johnson of his and his deputies' efforts and the result.

However, he waited until late afternoon to drive to the coal mine to see Johnson. Locating the superintendent who had driven the father home the afternoon his wife had reported their son missing, Taylor explained the intensive search that had been carried out by him, his deputies and numerous townspeople. Due to the unfortunate results, he requested that Johnson be relieved of his duties a bit early.

"Sure, Sheriff," the superintendent replied as he wiped a smudge of coal dust off his chin. "I'm certainly sorry you couldn't find the boy. Terrible thing to have happen." He called to another man and said, "Get Johnson here."

Turning back to Taylor the man explained, "I know this will be hard on Johnson and his wife, but I just can't let him be off work much and still pay him. I can give him one or two more days with pay, but after that . . ." The sentence hung in midair.

"Understand your problem. Appreciate what you're doing, and I know Johnson and his wife will."

"Well, I've got kids myself, four actually, and my wife would go crazy if one of them got hurt or went missing . . . Oh, here's Johnson now."

Taylor explained to the father the lack of success in finding his son and that he would be taking him home so he could tell his wife. Johnson merely stared from the sheriff to the superintendent, unable or unwilling to fully comprehend Taylor's words. "He's still gone? You didn't find my boy?" the man asked, walking slowly toward the sheriff's car.

As the two drove the miles back toward Wallton, Johnson sat quietly, staring out the window. Taylor tried to ease the man's pain by explaining that he would keep searching, that the father should not give up hope of locating Bobby, that the boy would eventually be found or come home on his own.

However, Johnson seemed not to hear him, and the two drove through the gathering dusk. Finally, as his house came in sight, the father stirred, looked at Taylor and said quietly, "Thanks, Sheriff, but he's gone, you know. He's just gone. Won't never come home no more. Don't know how I'm gonna tell my wife. She keep thinking we'll find him."

———————◆◆◆———————

The next morning, Taylor made an appointment to see banker Allen. He was early, and as he waited for the man to complete some other business, he spoke quietly with Barbara Hersey.

"Don't suppose you'd consider going out with me . . . to dinner . . . or to a movie?"

"If you don't think I'd do that, why did you bring it up?" Barbara replied, laughing at him.

Damn woman! Actually damn most women. Taylor shook his head. He seldom swore, unless under great stress. However, when he came into contact with females, particularly young ones, he always seemed to make a fool of himself. At least he thought he did. *Why do women always make it so hard to have a conversation with them? Wonder if all men have the same problem I seem to have.*

"Well, if you are not too busy this coming Saturday night, would you like to go to a movie or have dinner with me? Does that sound better?"

Barbara Hershey smiled. "That sounds lovely, Sheriff, or should I just call you Mr. Taylor when we are dining together?"

Taylor promised that he would leave his job behind. "I'll check with you on Friday . . . just to make sure nothing has come up that would change my plans."

"You're talking about the missing boy?"

"Yes, we've done everything that can be done to locate him but just no luck so far. We're about to come to the conclusion that he jumped a coal train out of town."

"Was he having problems at school . . . at home?"

"No, and that's the funny part. He was doing all right in school, and his folks say there were no problems at home. I kinda believe them. They're really upset by this . . . especially the mother. The dad has his work to keep him occupied . . ."

"Good to see you again, Sheriff," Allen interrupted their conversation. "I've got a few minutes now before I need to make another phone call."

Immediately Taylor followed the man into his office and quickly explained his reason for the meeting.

"Wonder if you'd mind again putting up some reward money? Didn't help with the Gower girl murder but might bring something to light on this missing boy."

Allen said that the bank again would offer $500 reward for information about the Johnson boy and asked Taylor what he intended to do about the case.

"Just keep looking and hope something turns up," Taylor replied. "Not much else we can do." He thanked the banker for his continued support and as he started down the stairs whispered to Barbara Hershey that he would call her.

Nell Taylor was delighted when her son told her that he had asked Barbara Hershey for a date.

"I'm so glad. She's a fine woman . . . that pretty blonde hair . . . and well-educated for a woman. She's got a good job at the bank . . . is always courteous and friendly . . .has an excellent reputation . . . helps out with our bake sales at the church . . . really can bake a scrumptious pie . . ."

"Mother, stop! I'm just taking her out . . . I'm not marrying her. We're just going to a movie."

"Course she isn't all that young. That could be a problem . . . time for her to think about having babies . . . better to have them young than waiting 'til you're old . . ."

Taylor closed the outside door quietly. He wasn't certain that his mother realized that he was no longer in the house. He knew that she would continue thinking about Barbara Hershey, putting up good points next to any bad points. Taylor could think of no bad points except, as his mother had indicated, Barbara Hershey was in her mid-twenties. In Wallton that was consider extremely old for an unmarried women.

Taylor smiled. Here he was getting close to thirty-three, and he didn't consider himself to be old. However, he supposed his mother was right. If Barbara Hershey planned on having a family, she ought to be thinking seriously of getting married and settling down. However, he was not contemplating Barbara settling down with him . . . just some vague unknown individual . . . who would marry her and give her a home and kids.

———————◆———————

The next day Taylor called Barbara and suggested that they see a movie the coming Saturday night. "If that's all right with you," was the way he put it. He had thought over his hasty chat with her the previous day and realized that taking her to dinner would involve making conversation for several hours. He was not comfortable with that thought. What could they talk about? He couldn't discuss much about his job and felt that she couldn't discuss the bank's business. That probably would lead to some awkward silences. A movie was safer. Most people sat quietly during the film. Solving that problem in his mind, he decided that if the two seemed compatible, he would consider calling her for dinner at a later time.

The movie evening turned out well. The film, *Barbary Coast* with Edward G. Robinson, had been fairly good, and Barbara and he seemed to find some common ground for later discussion of the plot. Walking her to the door of her parent's home, Taylor said he would call her when he had another free weekend. He explained that every other weekend he released one of the deputies and took his shift. The men usually had to work at least six and sometimes seven days or nights a week, as did Taylor if some unusual problem came up.

"We all work as many nights as it takes when something comes up that has to be taken care of," he had explained, hoping that, unlike his previous fleeting involvement with Agnes Parsons, Barbara would understand. "Sometimes I have to cancel an appointment."

She indicated that she understood, and Taylor made an effort to see Barbara at least once a month for an evening out. Thanksgiving, Christmas, the New Year slipped by with the two of them occasionally showing up at various functions. He had heard from one source that his mother had told her circle of friends that she felt "something is going to come out of this."

Nevertheless, Taylor and his deputies had been extremely busy, and he found that he had little free time and was often too tired for an evening of pleasure. As usual, winter weather brought on numerous problems, many of them of a minor nature. Someone was ill with no one to help out; someone did not have adequate food or fuel; someone desperately needed transportation to the grocers, the doctor, the church. It also seemed like there was a never ending call for help with the sheriff and his men quickly responding to any reports of a crime, minor or serious. While Barbara Hershey's face occasionally crept into his mind during a busy day, it was only a fleeting vision.

"Someone in there to see you, Sheriff," Alma said shortly after one o'clock Friday on an early April afternoon. "Some man. Been waiting for quite a spell. Won't say what it's about . . . Been waiting about an hour and a half. Didn't know where you were . . ."

"No problem, Alma." Taylor smiled at the criticism in the woman's voice. "I'll get right with him."

Taylor took off his gloves as he walked toward his office. He had been out checking with a woman who thought she had seen someone stealing firewood from a neighbor's yard. January, February and March all had been extremely cold, snowy months, and Taylor was not surprised that someone would need to steal fuel in order to stay warm.

"Still a bit chilly out there for April," Taylor said as he nodded at the man who had risen when he entered. He hung his coat across the back of the chair, sat down behind his desk, and indicated that the man should take a seat. "Now, what can I do for you?"

"Don't think we've ever met, Sheriff.," the man began. "I'm Sam Ansell. Live over on the north edge of town . . . got a room with a family there . . . the Harrods."

While waiting, Ansell had removed his coat and gloves and held in his lap a battered hat, its brim faded with sweat at the edges. A middle-aged man with watery blue eyes and hair still dark brown, he was perched cautiously on the edge of the chair.

"Not sure I know the Harrods . . . can't know everybody. You got a problem with them?" Taylor was not surprised that the Harrods had rented out a room as any money coming into a household would be welcome.

"No! No, they're good people." Ansell waited hesitantly before continuing. "I'm working out at the Fair Grounds . . . lucky enough to pick up a little work . . . Well, me and two other guys . . . we're tearing down those old bleachers . . ."

"The old wooden bleachers on the east side of the horse arena?"

"Right, Sheriff." Again Ansell hesitated before saying, "We think we've found a body . . . or what's left of a body."

"What do you mean? You think it's a body?"

"Well, we could see some rags . . . parts of clothing, I guess. What looked like a bone . . . We didn't want to touch it. Thought we'd better get up here right away and tell you . . ."

"Good!" Taylor responded. "You did exactly right. I'll have Alma find one of my deputies, and you and I will go down there now. You can show me what you think you've found."

Taylor grabbed his coat and, after telling Alma to try and locate Deputy Musso, the two men got into Taylor's car and drove toward the fair grounds. Arriving there, Taylor found the other two workers standing away from the bleachers, stomping their feet to keep them warm. Although most of the previous snow had melted due to an unusual late winter drizzle, the ground was soggy and cold, and Taylor noted that neither of the men wore heavy shoes. All three probably considered themselves lucky to be employed.

Only Ansell followed Taylor toward one end of the bleachers as Taylor looked around at the stacks of old lumber. He recalled sitting and watching calf roping at the County Fair and ball games during the school year. One had to be extra careful sitting on the bleachers as the rough wood had splinters which could make their way through the seat of a pair of Levis.

Taylor crawled into what was left of the crumbling structure and found crammed back in one corner the pile of rags Ansell had mentioned. He could see what had disturbed the three men. Poking out of the pile was what appeared to be a hand with stubs of fingers.

Inching back out of the space, Taylor told Ansell to go and wait with the other men until his deputy arrived. "Shouldn't be too long. You tell him that I've gone to get Doctor Mason. Now, don't you three go back near there! Just wait for me to return."

Ansell nodded that he understood and headed back toward the other workmen. As Taylor drove away, he could see Musso coming toward the Fair Grounds. Flagging him down, Taylor briefly told him what had been discovered and that he was going to get the doctor and alert the funeral home. Musso nodded and indicated that he would wait with the three men until Taylor and the doctor arrived.

"Hate to say it, but I'm getting too old for this kind of thing," Mason said as he straightened up. He had crawled back into the bleachers and examined some of the bits of clothing which still clung to the small body. Then he had called to Taylor to have the workers disconnect some more of the boards so that the bones could be removed as intact as possible.

"Couldn't tell much back in that corner," Mason said, frowning a little and rubbing his shoulders. "Pretty sure some animals have been at the body. Probably rats or maybe even cats and dogs. Too cold for most dogs or cats to have been out for any length of time this past winter so most likely rats. Eating would have begun a few days after death."

"What caused the boy's death, Doc?"

"Can't say for sure but my guess would be a hit on the head. Won't be able to tell exactly until we get him out of there. Know he's frozen now, but that don't tell us much. From the looks of it, he's probably been in that corner for quite a spell. Been there ever since he went missing last year would be my guess. Doubt that he would have just crawled in there to die. Maybe got hurt somehow crawling around the seats and just couldn't get out. Might have yelled but who would have heard him? Not many people around here except during the summer when the County Fair is going. Oh, here comes O'Connor and the hearse. Let's wait and see what Will says."

O'Connor eventually would provide autopsy results, but Taylor was impatient. He wanted to hear the mortician's immediate assessment as to the cause of death. He thought Mason might be wrong about the strangulation and that the boy might just have frozen to death. If that were the case, he wanted it confirmed. Then the question would be why the boy had crawled voluntarily into the bleachers and just stayed there, stayed there for months? Was he hiding from something? Had he not eaten anything, simply died of starvation? The questions raced through Taylor's mind.

"Head wound," O'Connor" stated after a cursory examination of the body. "Agree with Doc. Didn't just starve to death," the mortician continued. "Skull cracked. Must have been something heavy to do that damage. Also appears that his arm was broken. Can't tell if the injury to the head came first or if the arm was broken first, maybe as he tried to get away."

"If the hit on the skull was hard enough to cause death, then why would someone need to break the arm?" Taylor asked. "Arm must have been broken first when the kid was grabbed."

"True. Probably grabbed hard and then hit." O'Connor looked from Taylor to the doctor. "Must have been put there the day he went missing. Most of his clothes rotted out because of being wet. You remember, had an unusual amount of rain during October and then the winter snows . . ." O'Connor stopped speaking and just looked at the other two men. "Who's gonna let his folks know?"

For a minute Taylor didn't seem to comprehend O'Connor's question. His concentration had been about who might have killed the boy and when. Now he looked at the mortician and Mason and shook his head.

"I'll be the one to do it. Nearly five months they've wondered what happened to their son. Thought he had jumped a train; now I'll have to tell them he was killed . . . killed right here in town just a few miles from his house."

"Need me to go with you?" Mason asked quietly. "I can get back to my patients later."

"Yeh, Doc. I'm not sure how hard his folks are gonna take this . . . particularly his mother. You come along in case I need you, but you can go back to your doctoring now. I won't go out there until this evening when the father's done with work and may be home. I'll come and get you at your office. Won't make any difference now when I tell them. Won't help any."

———————◆◆———————

It was dark when the two men drove into the Johnson's yard. Almost immediately the door opened and Sam Johnson poked his head out.

"That you, Sheriff?"

"Yes, it is Mr. Johnson, and Dr. Mason is with me."

"Well, get yourselves in here out of the cold. Get something to warm yourselves up. Got coffee, and there's soup left over from supper. Think it's still warm. If not, wife can heat it up for you in a minute."

Johnson closed the door as the two men entered and offered to take their coats. Lucy Johnson turned from the stove where she was ladling stew from a pot into a large bowl, and the two boys were already sitting at a table. From the expression on her face, Taylor could see that she knew why the two men were there.

"Oh, no! No!" was all she moaned, but the anguish in her voice reached her husband, who realized the two men were not there for a friendly visit.

"Sorry, ma'am," Taylor said and turned to the father. "We . . . actually some workmen found your boy."

Johnson continued to stand near the door and stared at Taylor as though he had been speaking in a foreign language. Finally, he shook himself and asked, "You just found him? After all of these months? Where's he been staying?"

"He ain't staying nowhere," his wife said shrilly. "He's dead. Don't you understand why they're here? Bobby's dead. He's gone now forever. Ain't no chance he's coming home." Tears poured down her face, but without any noise, merely silent weeping.

Suddenly Johnson comprehended what his wife had said. He stood stunned for a moment, his eyes staring blindly at both men. Finally he said softly, "We'll want to see our boy, Sheriff. Need to see him. Need to see he's put away properly."

Taylor wasn't certain what to say . . . wasn't sure that there was a way he could explain delicately that the body was in no condition for anyone to see . . . especially not his mother. After over six months with rain, snow, freezing temperatures and animals gnawing on the body, the boy would not look anything like his parents remembered.

What had made Mason and Taylor certain that it was Bobby Johnson was the size of the body and the blonde hair lying tangled around the skull. The clothing had lost all of its color and had begun to rot so that much of it was merely tatters. Under a shirt collar could be seen faint checks of red and blue. Taylor wanted to ask the mother if her son wore a shirt that color but decided it was unimportant. The father should be able to tell if it were his son.

"Like you to come with us, Mr. Johnson," Taylor said. "Up to the funeral parlor. No need for your wife to leave your other two boys alone. I'll bring you back home."

"Fine. Fine." Johnson said abruptly. He went to his wife, patted her on the shoulder and said, "Won't be long, Ruthie."

Ruthie Johnson didn't respond, merely looked blankly at her husband, nodded her head, and continued standing at the stove, the large spoon clutched tightly in her hand.

"We'll wait in the car," Mason said as he and Taylor started to walk from the room. "Take your time, Mr. Johnson. There's plenty of time."

Robert "Bobby" Johnson, age eleven, was buried at nine thirty in the morning two days later near the edge of the ten acres where his parents lived. It was a raw day with a steady wind threatening to drop rain from low-hanging gray clouds. The coffin was a little more than just a pine box but not much more. Will O'Connor had lowered the price substantially, and both Mason and Taylor had chipped in to help with the cost. Johnson had told Jenkins that he would pay off "any extra" over the next year.

"Can't afford anything better," Johnson had explained to all three men. Guess it doesn't matter much 'cept I want his mother to know I did my best."

The mourners, huddled against the cold, were small in number – the family, the Hanson cousins, the coal mine superintendent, Taylor and one of his deputies, and a few close neighbors. Dr. Mason was too occupied with patients to attend but had arranged for a small wreath of pine branches to be made for the coffin, and a neighbor had contributed a few pink blossoms from a geranium plant that was kept indoors and had continued blooming during the winter months.

Reverend Parsons conducted the service, a quick, simple one as the group stood in the brisk March breeze. Taylor, along with one of his deputies, slowly followed the neighbors and the Johnsons into their house. Several women, Taylor's mother included, had sent cinnamon rolls and biscuits for those wishing a bite of breakfast after the burial, and two large pots of coffee were on the stove. Reverend Parsons moved solemnly among the mourners and eventually came to stand by Taylor, merely nodded and said, "Sheriff."

Taylor was a bit uncomfortable by the man's short greeting and attributed it to his previous connection with the man's daughter. Possibly the reverend thought that Taylor had not given Agnes Parsons the proper amount of attention the few times the two had dated.

"Perhaps, I'm just imagining it," Taylor thought. "Perhaps the minister is merely displeased because I always seem too busy to attend church services.

As he and the deputy drove back into Wallton, Taylor recalled a brief conversation with Mr. Johnson about his other two boys. The oldest, at just past age six, should be starting school after the coming summer. However, he would be too young to walk by himself into Wallton, even if his parents would permit it.

"Always thought Bobby would be here to walk with him," Johnson had explained when Taylor raised the question. "Guess he'll have to start at home the way Bobby did. The missus has more schooling than me. She can read and write better. She's already taught my boy his letters and numbers up to fifty, and he can read a bit. Still got some of the books left by Bobby when he was younger. Maybe she can get him started on those."

"That should help for a while," Taylor said, adding that he would ask if the school would let the Johnson's borrow books used in the first grade.

"Appreciate that, Sheriff, and appreciate all you've done for us. I've got my job which is a blessing and lets me and the missus keep our property."

Taylor had looked out over the few acres of Johnson land and again thought how barren it was, some scrub grass that might help feed the horses. Although Mrs. Johnson already had started her small vegetable garden, she had to tote pails of water from the well to keep it barely moist. The stalks of a few early onions were curling at the top and showing patches of brown at their tips. Taylor thought perhaps she would have better luck if she planted only a couple hills of summer squash. Two hills of squash would be less to water, and the cookedvegetable with a bit of butter and salt would add to what he suspected often were meager meals.

Back at the office, Taylor tried to keep busy with paperwork, but he couldn't concentrate. He could still see the anguish in the eyes of the Johnsons as clods of earth hit the small coffin.

Another kid dead. No reason for it. Someone here killed that boy. Don't have any idea who. Just like the Gower girl. Has to be someone local. I know I'm right. Doc agrees with me. Has to be someone who lured the kid, someone who usually wouldn't frighten a child . . . someone living right here in Wallton . . . out and about like all of us . . . But why? What causes someone to kill a child? What could kids do that would make someone mad enough to kill them?

He stared out his open office door at Alma sitting as usual in her dark skirt and blouse, doing paperwork and answering phone calls. She must have sensed his scrutiny for she suddenly looked up. "Need something, Sheriff?

"No! No, Alma, just thinking and you were in my line of vision."

"Well, I know you got a lot on your mind what with another killing. Yell, if you want something . . . more coffee . . . anything."

Taylor nodded and abruptly got up. He needed to get out of the office but didn't know where he could go and not encounter questions about the reason for the Johnson boy's death. Going home was not an option – too many questions there. As usual Mason would be swamped with patients and, Taylor knew, could add nothing to help his dilemma. He got in his car and drove aimlessly up and down the streets.

Eventually he ended up at the Fair Grounds. By now the bleachers had been totally removed, the fence to which they had been attached standing unsteadily in the background. Only a few remnants of the wooden seats remained as those still in good shape had been sold to a local lumber yard. Wood, even old used wood, could bring a hefty price. Taylor sat for over a half hour, merely staring out the window. A bit of sun occasionally poked lean fingers through the clouds and threw shadows across the yard.

Taylor realized that Bobby Johnson had not walked down to the old bleachers himself; someone had brought him there. He would have been too heavy to carry any distance, so he was either killed there or transported from some distance in an automobile. A fair number of families in Wallton owned cars; the vehicle could have belonged to any of them. Carrying or possibly just dragging the body up to the corner of the seats where it was found would have required some strength, so Taylor felt the perpetrator would not have been feeble.

"It's got to be a man," Taylor said aloud. He was certain the killer was male, but that didn't help much. Quite a number of local men didn't have steady jobs and were out and about all day. Many of them probably owned an auto even if they hardly had money for gasoline. Try as he might, he simply couldn't see any way to find the individual who killed Bobby Johnson and, he was now certain, the other children buried in the Wallton cemeteries.

————◆•◆•◆————

The weeks and months rolled past, and almost before Taylor knew it, his mother's annual New Year's party was in full swing. "Happy New Year was boisterously called out heard as the clock struck midnight, and another year began. Guests spoke about space being added to the J. C. Penney store, about a local boy who had now completed his college degrees and become a lawyer, about a few more jobs becoming available, about the disturbing news coming out of Europe of a possible war. Yet, for the most part, everyone seemed to feel that 1938 would be a good year.

Nell Taylor, now in her mid-fifties continued to be in good health as did her son. In July Taylor would be up for re-election as sheriff, but he was certain that he would win. So far, there was no one running against him, and he doubted there would be.

Taylor's and the deputies' workload remained constant. Unfortunately, both Sam Musso and Arnold Drury were beginning to show their ages. Musso had been off work for nearly two months after hernia surgery the past year, and Drury, now sixty-two, was slowing down. At the next County Commissioners' meeting, Taylor would ask for additional money to hire two new men. Hopefully, the commissioners would be sympathetic and grant him enough funds to at least hire one. This would ease the hours all the other deputies needed to work although it probably would have very little effect on his own workload.

Soon, he and Barbara Hershey would have been dating for over a year, and Taylor knew he should either make a commitment or stop seeing her. For the past few months his mother had stopped extolling Barbara's virtues, and this bothered him a little. He wouldn't ask, but he wondered if she heard or seen something about the woman that caused her to become more reluctant to prod her son into a marriage?

If he asked Barbara to marry him, and if she accepted which he felt she would, this created another problem. Where would they live? He could afford to rent, actually purchase, another home. Taylor knew if the couple did so, his mother would be very upset. When he eventually had broached the subject of marriage to Barbara, she insisted that the couple could continue living with her.

"It's about time you decided to marry, and there's plenty of room here," Nell Taylor had declared as the two sat on their screened back porch. "Probably Barbara will keep her job at the bank until the first baby comes, and then I'll be able to help her care for the child. It will make things much easier for her to have another woman to help out. Babies take a lot of care."

Babies! Taylor had not really thought about children. He had been reared as an only child and had never been around small children. He also felt that living with his mother would not be the best thing for Barbara Hershey . . or him. Two women in the same household could create problems. The more his mother gushed about his possible marriage and the living arrangements, the more determined Taylor became to remain a bachelor.

Unless Barbara terminated it, he would just let his relationship with her continue as it had been. They were not the lovers portrayed in novels and movies, although there had been times when they had shared some passionate kisses, actually a bit more than passionate. Barbara always seemed to know when to draw the line on romance. They would go out whenever he was free, and she made no demands on is time. She seemed to accept his dedication to his job. He hoped their present arrangement would continue to be satisfactory with her; however, he felt certain that she and her parents expected more.

———————————————

Driving back into Wallton on a late May afternoon, Taylor noticed Ruthie Johnson heading out of town. Carrying what appeared to be a heavy grocery sack, she was walking and pulling behind her a small wagon containing her two boys. Swinging the car around, Taylor pulled across the highway and blocked her path.

"Mrs. Johnson. It's hot out here. Let me give you and the boys a lift out to your place."

"Oh, I couldn't put you out, Sheriff," the woman replied as she pushed a swath of damp hair off her forehead. "Besides you and your momma have done more than enough for us, and you were headed the other way."

Taylor was not certain to what she was referring. Other than his attending her son's burial, Nell Taylor had baked some cinnamon rolls for the Johnson family, To Taylor that was little enough to do for a grieving household.

"Won't put me out at all," Taylor said. "You need to get in from this heat. He loaded the two boys, the wagon and the sack of groceries into the back seat of the car. Sighing, Ruthie Johnson began climbing into the front seat, wincing as she moved her right leg so that Taylor could shut the door.

"Leg hurt?" Taylor asked as they started out of town.

"Just a tad. Pulled something when I was trying to get down a bale of hay for the horses."

"Do you or Mr. Johnson ride the horses? I don't recall ever seeing him riding into town."

"No. Don't ride them. Don't know why he has them. Think it makes him feel important. Other people will think he's not poor . . . can afford to keep horses just for show."

Taylor nodded and thought for a minute about what Ruthie Johnson had said. Even though the small Johnson property was a sorry piece of land to Taylor's way of thinking, Levi Johnson was financially able to own acreage. Well, ten acres. He was employed at the mines, and he also could own and feed horses. Taylor could understand to some degree that in Johnson's mind, the husband and father saw himself as a successful man.

"Well, the boys may learn to ride them when they are older," Taylor said, and then turned the conversation to the hot weather and the lack of rainfall. He was glad that Ruthie Johnson avoided talking about her dead son or asking whether he had discovered who had committed the murder.

The night of the 4th of July a woman killed her husband. The couple had walked to a local bar, gotten into an argument, and the wife had gone back home. When the husband arrived several hours after midnight, thoroughly inebriated, the two had argued, and he had slapped her. Grabbing a pistol which her husband always kept loaded, she had shot him twice, once in his chest and once in the face.

Taylor was awakened from sleep by a deputy who explained the problem. Then Taylor called Mason who alerted O'Connor, and all three arrived at the crime scene. The doctor pronounced the husband dead; the mortician toted the body out of the house; the wife admitted shooting him. Everything seemed cut and dried. However, Taylor had a problem – what to do with the wife.

Wallton's jail did not have facilities to house a woman. In fact, neither Mason nor O'Connor could recall a Wallton female ever needing to be taken to the jail. Finally, Mason agreed that the woman could be housed for the rest of the night in the town's hospital. One of the deputies would stay with her, and the next day Taylor would get her moved to a cell in a town to the north.

"Hospital should be like a fairytale place to her after living here," Mason said as he waited for Taylor to lock up the house.

Taylor nodded. The house, if it could be called a house, consisted of two adobe rooms, each with one tiny window. A double bed was in one room, and the other, which Taylor thought must be a kitchen, was furnished with a small cheaply made wooden table and two chairs, the back of one coming loose from the seat. In one corner was a cast iron stove with a small shelf clinging to the wall and holding a few blue and white dishes. Along the other wall was a box with a tub on top, and Taylor assumed it served as a sink in which to wash dishes or do laundry. The house smelled of stale food and dirty laundry. All in all, it was a dismal place . . . *not fit for humans,* Taylor thought.

By the time the two men left the hovel, it was nearly 5 a.m., and Mason suggested Taylor come home with him. "I'll put on coffee and scare up some breakfast," was the way he put it.

Taylor was quick to agree. Although he knew his mother would be up and in her kitchen shortly, he didn't wish to discuss the murder with her. Later in the day he'd go over every detail for her.

The two men sat in companionable silence after downing coffee. Crisp bacon and pancakes with butter and honey.

"You're a really good cook, Doc," Taylor declared and then realized that Mason had to be since his wife was dead, and he was alone.

"Doc Mason's on the line for you, Sheriff," Alma called to Taylor, exasperation in her voice . "Won't tell me what it's about. Just said for you to get on quick."

Taylor picked up the phone, thinking it was odd that the physician would be calling him near the middle of the morning. Usually it was Taylor who called the doctor for some sort of information. Of course, the two met occasionally for a hurried meal.

"Looking for someone to buy you a late breakfast . . . or lunch, Doc?" Taylor asked.

"No!" came the harsh reply.

"What's the problem?" Taylor realized immediately that it was not a social call.

"Better get up to George Allen's home right now. Don't say anything to anyone. Just come on up. I'll be waiting for you." The phone line went dead.

Grabbing his hat, Taylor walked out of his office and said to Alma. "Going to meet the doc. Tell anyone who wants me that I'll be going on to lunch. Be back in a little over an hour probably."

Arriving at the Allen residence, Taylor saw both Allen's and Mason's cars parked in front. He had never been in the Allen home although, like everyone in Wallton, he knew where it was and had driven past it numerous times over the years. Set on a small elevation, the prestigious house was a two-story, constructed of native limestone with a slate roof. Two large spruce trees hovered on each side of the brick walk leading to a wide veranda and a heavy oak door, its leaded glass windows etched with vines. The door opened as Taylor climbed the five steps leading up to it, and Mason quickly drew him inside.

"Come on in," Mason said quietly as he took Taylor's arm and walked him through a foyer and into a large living room, its windows hidden by maroon brocade drapes. "No one know you're here, right?"

"I didn't tell Alma, if that's what you mean," Taylor started to grin and then saw by the expression on Mason's face that something serious had occurred, and he was in no mood for levity.

"What's wrong? Tell me."

"Allen's dead!"

"Dead!" Taylor was stunned. "Dead when?"

"About a half hour ago as far as I can tell. His sister called the office. Told my nurse it was an emergency, and I came as soon as I could drive here."

"How?" Taylor continued to look at the doctor, confusion on his face.

"Shot himself." The doctor shook his head. "I couldn't believe it either. Took a shotgun and just about blew his head off. Come on upstairs. You'll want to see where it happened . . . see the body."

The two men walked up a wide staircase and into a large bedroom on the second floor. Lying near a window that looked out over Wallton was the body of George Allen, most of his face obliterated. Blood spattered a large portion of the room and dotted curtains and a white cotton bedspread.

"His sister . . ." Taylor asked. "His sister here?"

"Yes, she's sitting in a room downstairs at the back of the house, a sunroom I think they call it. She heard the shot and found him. As you can see, it is a mess. She's not in the best of shape right now."

"I don't doubt it," Taylor replied, still trying to make sense of what Mason was telling him and what he was seeing. "It is a mess, and I'm sure she's not in good shape. However, I'm gonna have to talk with her, Doc, see if she can give me some sort of explanation . . ."

"Well, when you do, be as easy on her as you can. You'll see that she's in shock . . . not saying anything . . . just sitting and staring into space. If you can postpone it, you can talk with her a little later. Right now, I need you to go and get the undertaker and bring him here. Don't call. Just go and get him so news of the death doesn't get out right now. I'd go, but someone needs to stay with Miss Allen. When you get back there'll be time enough to talk with her and to decide what to do about letting the news out."

Taylor left the house and drove to O'Connors' business. Taking the mortician aside, he quietly explained the reason that the man needed to come with him.

Like Taylor had been, Ted O'Connor was stunned by the news. "Dead," he had exclaimed. "Why Allen's only about sixty. Sister's about five years older. Sure it wasn't a heart attack?"

"No, Ted. He did it himself, but we don't want that out right now. I'm telling you all that we know. Want you to take care of everything for Miss Allen. Get the body moved . . . all that. We need to go now. Follow me with the hearse, please."

The two men found Mason waiting for them, and while the doctor stayed below, Taylor and the mortician carried a canvas stretcher upstairs. As the mortician draped a cloth over the body, Taylor noted the stunned expression on O'Connor's face and said, "Yeh, I know it's not something we'd expect to happen. Let me help you get him out to the hearse."

Both he and Mason helped load the body into the hearse, and Mason asked O'Connor to keep the incident quiet if he could.

"Okay, Doc," O'Connor agreed, "but I know some people saw me take the hearse out of the garage. Don't think they followed me, but I saw someone out in their yard just up this street. So you know there will be questions shortly. People know that I don't take the hearse out unless someone's dead. What can I do?"

"Delay answering your phone for an hour or so if you can. We don't want people calling or coming up here right now if we can help it."

As the mortician pulled away, Taylor and Mason hurried back into the Allen residence, and Mason led Taylor to the waiting Gwendolyn Allen. She was seated primly on a flower-upholstered sofa in an octagon-shaped room with windows on three sides. Her fluff of white hair fell haphazardly across her forehead, nearly concealing pale blue eyes. Dressed in a dark green robe, her hands clasped in her lap, she looked up as the two men entered and merely nodded at them.

Gwendolyn Allen did not appear to have been weeping, and Taylor thought that was odd. As far as he knew the banker – now the late banker – was her only relative . . . possibly the only person she saw daily. Like most of the town's residents, he was aware that she seldom left the home. In fact he couldn't recall having seen her any place in town in several years.

Trying to console the woman, he asked quietly, "Is there anything we can do for you, Miss Allen? Is there someone we can call . . . to come and stay with you?"

"Thank you, no, Sheriff. I'm quite able to stay by myself, and my housekeeper, Rachel, should be here shortly."

Taylor glanced over at Mason who quickly explained, "Miss Allen is referring to Rachel O'Leary. I think you may know the woman, Sheriff . . . married to Mike O'Leary . . works as a bartender."

Taylor nodded at the housekeeper, noting the formal tone in Mason's explanation. If he had questions of Mason, he felt he should also be more formal in front of the sister and refer to the man as Doctor instead of his usual form of address – Doc.

"Please sit down," Gwendolyn Allen said, motioning toward two small straight-backed wooden chairs with padded cushions. "I know you have to talk with me." She continued sitting with her head down, her hands folded neatly in her lap.

"Just a few quick questions now," Taylor said as he settled uncomfortably on a dainty chair. He didn't know quite how to begin.

"Can you think of any reason for your brother to do . . . this?" He didn't wish to say "kill himself" or "commit suicide," and he knew he was fumbling with his question.

Gwendolyn Allen replied quietly, "Who can know what is in a person's mind?"

Taylor thought that was an odd way for the woman to answer his question and decided to try something else. "I mean . . . did you know of any problems . . . health problems for instance?"

"Not that I knew. I thought my brother was quite healthy. Most of his problems with health had been in his youth, and those were dealt with. My parents always saw to our health. They took excellent care of us," she added sharply.

Taylor nodded and decided that he would take a different approach.

"No problems at the bank that you know of?" Taylor was aware from past experience with a couple of suicides that people didn't just get up one morning and decide to end it all.

"Definitely not, Sheriff! The bank is sound."

"That's good to know, Miss Allen. Wouldn't want people to think otherwise and start 'a run' on the bank's funds. Still, there must have been some major reason for your brother . . ."

"Hellooo, I'm here. Running just a little late. Stopped at the grocers." Rachel O'Leary gushed. A short red headed woman slightly overweight, she was trying to jockey two large grocery sacks and a large brown purse without losing any of the contents. Seeing the doctor and the sheriff with her employer, she gasped, "What's happened? Are you all right, Miss Allen?"

Immediately Mason took one of the grocery sacks and ushered Rachel O'Leary out of the room. Taylor could hear the telephone ringing in the entry hall and wondered if the neighbors had been alerted to the unusual activity at the Allen home. Miss Allen did not seem to notice the interruption and continued to sit placidly on the couch, merely looking at her hands which now were lying palm up in her lap.

"Probably need to wait to go on with the questions, if you can," Mason whispered as he came back onto the sun porch. "Doubt if she is fully aware . . . really realizes what her brother has done."

"If you think that's best, Doc."

Turning to Gwendolyn Allen, Taylor explained that he would want to talk with her at a later time He knew there would be many things she now would need to do to arrange burial for her brother.

As the two men walked toward the front door, Taylor said to Mason, "I'll wait until later today or tomorrow morning, Doc, but I'm gonna have to ask her a bunch more questions. Got to be some drastic reason for Allen to have done this. Maybe she can recall something he said . . . something he did. Maybe he was very ill and hadn't told her."

"If he had been sick, I think I would have known," Mason said curtly. "I was his doctor like I am for the rest of Wallton."

"Didn't mean to offend you, Doc. Just can't get my mind around why he would do something like this."

"Well, now that you mention it, he hasn't been to see me for a couple . . . well quite a long time. Three or four years, I think. Guess he could have been seeing a doctor up north . . . not wanting me to know . . ."

"Probably it," Taylor said quickly and then asked, "What about Miss Allen? Shouldn't we try to get someone to come here to the house?"

"Rachel's here," the doctor replied. "I'll talk with her, tell her to keep an eye on her employer. Maybe she can stay the night. I need to get to my office; bet there's already a room full of anxious patients. Probably a good idea for you to let them at the bank know before it gets out around town."

———————————

Taylor left the home and drove immediately to the First National Bank. It had been open for a few hours, and everything seemed normal. Apparently, news of the doctor and him being at the Allen's home had not yet become known although he was certain it soon would be. Walking quickly upstairs, Taylor told Barbara of the man's death but did not mention that it was suicide.

"Just need you to be prepared," he said, noting the shocked expression on her face. "You're sure to be flooded with calls as soon as the news gets around town. Don't say anything. Just tell them to call my office, and Alma will take their names."

"What?" Barbara finally asked. "What was wrong? He hasn't complained about being ill."

"I'll explain it all to you later. Right now I just need you to stay calm. You will get a lot of question but just say you have no answers."

"Should we close the bank?"

He wasn't certain that Barbara had the authority to close the bank but didn't know who had that authority. Now that Allen was dead, who would be in charge? His sister, probably. She was the heir, but . . .

"No, don't want the bank closed right now. Might get people upset. Just do business as usual. Still, if it needs to be closed, who can say to do so if it comes to that? Are you the person who can shut the doors?"

"I don't know," she answered meekly. "I don't think so. This has never happened before. Mr. Allen was always here . . . always took care of everything or told someone to do it. I don't think he was every ill." She shook her head and then said, "His sister probably could shut the bank or maybe Mr. Sanford could do it. He handles all of the loan work." By now tears were beginning, and she groped in her desk for a handkerchief.

"Sorry, Barbara, didn't mean to be so abrupt with this bad news. Can you call down to Mr. Sanford and ask him to come upstairs. I'll wait in Mr. Allen's office, if that's okay." Even though the man was dead, Taylor still used the formal address when referring to the deceased man.

At Barbara's frantic call, John Sanford rushed upstairs. He appeared totally confused by the news of Allen's demise but quickly recovered and asked what he could do to help the sheriff. Taylor explained that he felt it better if the bank continued business as usual.

"As soon as the news spreads around town, and it will spread quickly, the place will be overrun with customers wanting to know if their money is safe, wanting to know all about the death. I know you're shocked, probably sad as you've worked for Mr. Allen for many years. However, from what Miss Hershey tells me, you are now in charge. Just reassure people that their money is safe . . . that you don't know any more about the death then what they have heard. I know you can do this."

Sanford indicated that he would do as Taylor directed and, after instructing Barbara to forward all calls to him, rushed back downstairs. Finally, shaking her head, Barbara asked, "Why? What caused him to do it?

"I have no idea. I'm as confused as you . . . as Doc Mason is. I need to get back up to the Allen house, speak with his sister, see if she can give me some more information. I'll try to call you later. Maybe come by."

Taylor hurried down the stairs and then walked calmly through the lobby. So far everything appeared to be just another banking day. So far the bad news would still be a secret.

It was a little past noon, and Taylor stopped by home to grab a bite to eat. He knew he would probably be at the Allen home most of the afternoon. Now, he had to make a decision whether to tell his mother about Allen. Finally, he decided to do so.

"I'm flabbergasted," she said, her hand covering her mouth, he eyes wide. "What can I do?"

"Well, mother, and I mean this, do not tell anyone. The bad news will be out soon enough, but I don't want you to be the one to spread it."

"What if someone calls me and asks? What can I say?"

"Dammit, mother! Just say you don't know anything."

"Well, you don't have to swear at me. I'm your mother after all."

"I know, mother. I'm sorry." Taylor replied, patting her hand. He was sorry about his gruff words, never swore in her presence even if terribly frustrated. "I'm just under a great deal of pressure right now. I don't know any more than just what I told you."

"All right. I'll do as you ask, but I know people will think it odd that I don't know anything. After all, I live with the sheriff."

"That you do, mother. That's your cross to bear. Everyone thinks you have been told all the secrets . . . that you know all the facts. Wish you did; then maybe I wouldn't have unsolved crimes."

Although Taylor knew his mother wasn't placated by his comments, he felt she would do as he had asked. Kissing her on the cheek, he grabbed the half-eaten sandwich and rushed out the kitchen door. He needed to make a brief stop by the office and warn Alma to listen but not add to any gossip that might come in from townspeople. He knew the phone at the office would be ringing all afternoon.

"Perhaps that's a good thing," he thought. He felt that someone in Wallton might have some information, or at least an idea, why the banker had killed himself.

———•◆•———

It was nearly three o'clock by the time Taylor arrived back at the Allen home. He was surprised to see a large black wreath, the sign of a home in mourning, already on the front door. Wallton did not have a florist shop as especially now during The Depression people could little afford to purchase fresh flowers. It was customary that for funerals people brought flowers from their gardens to place on a casket or a grave.

Before he could knock on the door, Rachel O'Leary admitted Taylor and led him toward the back of the home.

"Miss Allen's back sitting in the sun room, Sheriff. She likes it better than any of the other places in the house."

Taylor merely nodded and followed the housekeeper down the hall. The late banker's sister was seated where she had been earlier in the day, knitting on what appeared to be a sweater. Taylor watched as her hands, colorless, nearly as white as her white hair, quickly moved the knitting needles through the green yarn. He wondered if she were making a scarf or a sweater, possibly intended as a Christmas gift for her brother . . . a brother who would never receive the gift.

"Please sit, Sheriff," she said as she had done earlier in the day. "I know you may have more questions. However, I doubt that I will be able to provide answers for you . . . answers that might help you. Would you like some tea?"

"Thank you, no, ma'am," Taylor replied, impressed by both her poise and her calm speech. He sat on the chair indicated and said, "I just have a few more questions that I need to ask."

"Certainly," she replied. Immediately she put the knitting aside and, placing her hands in her lap, gave him her full attention.

Taylor noted that she was now dressed in a black mourning dress, its pleats falling mid-calf. Near an ecru lace collar was a small brooch of white pearls.

Probably real pearls and set in real gold, Taylor thought. *If mother were here, she'd know. Obviously Miss Allen can afford the real* thing. *Might see if I can get a brooch for mother . . . for her birthday or Christmas . . . not real pearls, of course. . ..*

"Something wrong, Sheriff?"

He realized that he had been staring at the woman and replied quickly. "No, no. I was just thinking about your brother's death. I asked Doctor Mason if Mr. Allen had been ill, but Mason felt he was in good health."

"That is not entirely correct, Sheriff." Taylor was again aware of her almost overly formal speech. "I am afraid that I have not been totally honest with you." She paused, looked down at her hands and then continued.

"My brother had been to see a physician up north. Actually he had been under the care of the man for over six or seven years now. Although he never told me a great deal about the tests that were conducted, what the results were. . ." She stopped speaking for a minute and then continued, "I knew that the results were less than encouraging . . . actually much less than encouraging."

"So he was quite ill but still kept up his daily routine?"

"Yes. The bank meant everything to him. He had nothing else."

"He had you, ma'am."

"True, but that is not the same as having a family of one's own. As you must be aware, my brother never married." She gazed out the window for a moment and then continued.

"I'm certain you also were aware of his disfigurement. Every person in town was. It had always been with him. My parents got him as much medical help as they could, but only so much reconstruction could be done. He had trouble in school . . . oh, not with his studies . . . he was exceptionally bright . . . quick to learn anything. However, the other children in grade school teased him, made fun of him . . . called him a monster. He never had any friends. Came home sobbing many afternoons. Eventually my parents had tutors for him . . . for both of us actually. We learned a great deal, but neither of us ever had any close friends . . . well no friends at all."

Taylor merely nodded and then asked, "No close relatives either . . . someone you would like me to notify of the death?"

"No! My parents were cousins . . . met and married, kept the money in the family, I guess." She smiled slightly. "Any relatives would be back in the East, and we never really kept in touch except for an occasional card at Christmas. After my parents died, it was just my brother and me. I took care of him, made certain he had good food, took any medication."

"The medicine must have been working," Taylor shifted his position on the chair. I hadn't heard that he wasn't at the bank as usual."

"Oh the bank was his life, his total life. I think it kept him sane, but he wasn't a happy man, Sheriff, nor a well man. Night after night I would hear him pacing around his bedroom or I'd find him downstairs just gazing out a window. I'd ask him what was wrong . . . what he was looking for, if there was something I could do to help him, but he always said, 'You can't help me, Gwen. No one can help me.' Isn't that odd?"

Taylor thought the comment from her brother was odd but said nothing, and Gwendolyn Allen didn't seem to notice. She had told him, actually poured out, the sad story of her brother's life. Uncomfortable and at a loss for how to respond, Taylor finally asked, "Can I help you make the funeral arrangements?"

"No, thank you. I had Sarah call Mr. O'Connor again, and he will be here tomorrow morning. I plan on having a small private service, just me and Sarah . . . a closed casket. I know my brother would like that. He wouldn't want anyone staring down at him . . . you know, the awful way he looked."

"Well, if there is anything you do need, please call my office," Taylor said as he got up. He knew she was referring to her brother's scarred face but could think of no way to respond. "I could be up here to help in a few minutes."

Gwen Allen walked him to the front door, and he was surprised not only at how small she was but at how frail she looked. His mother would have said, "A good stiff wind could blow her away." Taylor thought that was an accurate assessment.

Two days later, on a hot, cloudy June afternoon with rain threatening, Banker George Allen was carried to his grave by Will O'Connor and five other men who occasionally worked for the mortician. Reverend Parsons said a few words and recited the 23rd psalm as Gwendolyn Allen and Sarah O'Leary stood nearby and watched the coffin lowered into the grave. The entire ceremony took only a few minutes, and the two women walked silently back to the empty home. Taylor had parked his car near a fence at the back of the cemetery, watched the brief burial, and thought about what his mother had said when he told her there would be no formal services.

"Buried him just like a dog," she had exclaimed. He deserved better than that. He was important to our town."

Nell Taylor was correct in one aspect. George Allen and the bank had been a vital part of the town's life. Taylor wondered about the fate of the First National Bank now that its owner was dead. He realized that the sister would be Allen's heir and had heard from Barbara Hershey that Gwendolyn Allen intended to continue the bank's operation as her brother had done. All employess were to be retained, and an out-of-town attorney, one Walter L. Jefferson, would be handling all of the necessary legal work. It appeared that life in Wallton would go on as usual.

———◆•◆•◆———

July and August brought blistering heat to Wallton. An occasional sparse rain did little to dampen the ground or cool the temperature. Tempers were short at homes, businesses and the sheriff's office. Like the office, Taylor's home was hot. Although they had two fans to cool the air, Taylor's mother cooked only in the early morning, making meals that could be served cold during the rest of the day.

Minor altercations between family members occurred frequently around the town and out into the county. Children got into fights with other children; husbands and wives quarreled, often leading to blows and a call for police intervention; office workers were testy and short with customers; Taylor had to remind Alma and his deputies to always be polite but to use caution when dealing with the public's complaints.

"Know it's really warm, has been for quite a spell now. Know people may use harsh language. Just try and remember that, like you, they're hot and uncomfortable. They're probably taking out their frustration on you 'cause they've got no one else to blame for the heat. Try and be pleasant if at all possible."

The one place that was fairly cool, due to several large oscillating fans, was the theater. Saturday afternoon and all evenings except Sunday, the place was packed with anyone who did not have to work and who had the price of admission – 10 cents for children below age thirteen and twenty-five cents for adults.

"By and large, it's been a pleasant summer, mother," Taylor commented one evening as the two sat late into the evening. A quick summer rain squall had cooled the early September heat. The two drank iced tea which his mother made in large quantities, and Taylor enjoyed a second helping of his mother's rice pudding. He had always been fond of her recipe for rice pudding, made heavy with raisins and pecans and served cold with a bit of whipped cream.

"Wish I could eat like you do," his mother commented. "Getting gat so have to watch my weight."

Taylor didn't comment. As far as he could tell, Nell Taylor had not added an ounce to her normal weight. She had never been fat and, he thought, probably would never be fat. However, he knew she wasn't expecting an answer.

Changing the subject, he mentioned that Mason told him there had been an outbreak of whooping cough. "School's not open yet, so he doesn't know why the cases. Not too many yet but enough that the doc asked Mel Allen to put a word of caution in the *Wallton Weekly*. Think he's asked him to also mention the danger for kids to be down at the creek."

"Won't do any good, but I guess if people's warned, they can't complain later."

Taylor agreed and set his dish on a nearby step. Both he and his deputies tried to go down to the creek several times a day and shoo kids out of the water. However, as soon as they drove away, the kids returned. So far, the only problems Doc mason had to deal with were a broken arm and several incidents of feet cut on some sharp rocks. The town didn't need another badly injured or dead child down at the creek!

Labor Day came and went; school started; the weather cooled somewhat, and from Taylor's standpoint as sheriff, Wallton was fairly peaceful. He was even considering, seriously now, the prospect of proposing to Barbara Hershey.

Then four months after her brother's suicide, Gwendolyn Allen was dead. Apparently she he had simply cut her wrists, gone to sleep and never awakened. Discovered in her bed by Rachel O'Leary, the frightened woman had alerted Mason's office, and the doctor had immediately gone up to the Allen home.

Called by the doctor, Taylor had once again drove to the Allen home and was taken upstairs by Rachel O'Leary whose eyes were red from weeping.

"Look at her, "the physician said, "so much blood. She must have gotten into bed as usual, slit both of her wrists up toward her elbows. Didn't just slice across the wrist bone. That might not have done much good. Might not have bled enough . . . just seeped out and coagulated. If not, then it would have taken her a great deal of time to die."

Taylor knew Mason was correct. Gwen Allen's body was saturated with blood. However, when Mason tugged the bedspread up to the woman's face and concealed the gore, it appeared that she was merely asleep peacefully under a coverlet of pale lavender sprinkled with tiny white blossoms.

"Why, Doc?" Suicide . . . like her brother. The two of them. Why do you think she did it . . . followed him?

"Not certain we'll ever know. Still don't know why George Allen did it. Both of them strange people . . . lonely people, no family, no friends . . . no one to talk to. Living here by themselves, just the two of them, no contact for him outside the bank, no contact for her except with him or the housekeeper. Enough to make you want to kill yourself, I guess.

"Probably right, Doc, but just seems very, very strange to me. Neither of them too old. Lot of people still living who are considerably older than them. Plenty of money, nice house. I could understand him with that face, but just don't understand her doing the same thing."

Mason merely sighed and nodded in agreement.

"Who'll make the funeral arrangements?" Taylor asked abruptly.

"Hadn't thought about that." Mason looked at the sheriff, a perplexed expression on his face. "Guess I'll have to do it. No one else left except Rachel, and she's in pretty bad shape right now."

"O'Connor will need payment, Doc. Can't you contact the lawyer she used when she sold the bank. He probably needs to know she's gone."

"Right," Mason replied. "I'll get on it later today. Get her put away properly."

As he had indicated, Mason quickly contacted Gwendolyn's lawyer, explained the circumstances of her death, and received permission to handle all of the funeral arrangements. Three days later on blustery October morning, the last of Wallton's Mason family was buried with only Mason, the Reverend Parsons and Rachel O'Leary as the sole mourners.

Taylor did not attend the ceremony but sat in his car outside the gate. He felt he needed to do that if only as a sign of respect for the woman. The walnut casket and open grave with its waiting pile of dark earth contrasted sharply with the bare cottonwoods and the scattered leaves, now rapidly changing from gold to a faded brown.

Parsons and the other two bowed their heads for a prayer, and as the revered closed his *Bible,* both Mason and Rachel quickly turned away. Taylor immediately started the car; he did not wish to meet Mrs. O'Leary or Mason and engage in any conversation. He had not been a friend of the family and what continued to bother him was the question of why both of the Allen siblings would have committed suicide.

In January 1938, five days years after New Year began, the mailman brought Taylor a large envelope. It was from George Allen's Chicago lawyer. The man explained in a cover letter that he had taken care of all of the business arrangements for Gwendolyn Allen, had been able to contact one of the distant relatives about the home, and was in the process of listing the property for sale.

He further explained that the banker had left the enclosed letter with the lawyer's firm four years previously. Allen's instructions were that the letter was not to be sent to Taylor nor was it to be opened by anyone other than Taylor until the death of both George and his sister, Gwendolyn. Taylor unsealed the letter, immediately noting with interest the signature. Heavy cream-colored stationery embossed at the top with the initials GEA was covered with neat script written in black ink. Taylor carefully read the two pages several times.

Dear Sheriff Taylor:

You will not get this letter until both my sister and I are dead. Since my sister may live a good many more years, I hope you still will be the elected sheriff for Wallton and the surrounding county. I have always thought you were doing an excellent job. You were most considerate when meeting and talking with me, although our infrequent encounters were always more or less professional. Still, when I thought of you, it was as a friend.

Being in your profession of law enforcement, I realize that you are often in contact with deaths which are impossible to understand or solve. Such has been the case for you with the children killed in Wallton over the past fifteen or twenty years, including those that occurred before you were elected as sheriff.

I killed those children, Sheriff Taylor, all of them. I killed them, or contributed to their deaths in various ways over the years and have little remorse at having done so. The only one I regret is the small girl who was discovered in the creek. All of the boys deserved what they got. They taunted me mercilessly whenever I was outside of the bank and around town. Like the children with whom I went to grade school, they called me "the monster." When that continued to happen over the years, I simply had to punish those individuals.

The exception was the little girl. I do regret having killed her. When I saw her at the edge of the alley behind her home, I got out of my car and offered her a piece of candy. I meant only to be nice to her and give her the candy. She looked at me and gave a small laugh. Still that laughter brought on the rage I always felt. I strangled her, put her in my car and left her body in the creek. For that one incident, I am truly sorry.

As you might have been aware, I had been going to Chicago several times each month. These trips were not of a business nature but were to see a doctor. He was a doctor who specialized in problems of the mind. During the sessions I had with him, he became aware of my killing and tried to help me stop, urged me to confess. However, that would have meant my going to prison for the remainder of my life, or worse. It also would have caused my sister, Gwendolyn, extensive grief. I simply refused to take the doctor's advice, and as you know, my reason for visiting him and my problems were kept confidential.

Unfortunately for her, my sister surmised that I had been doing the murders. However, she never confronted me with the that knowledge, so I can only assume that she suspected or knew truth. Please do not blame her for not bringing her supposition to your attention. I was her only living relative, and she punished herself by becoming a recluse.

If you, or anyone who follows you as sheriff, should choose to make this letter public (but only after Gwendolyn is deceased), please feel free to do so. Perhaps Mel Dawson will publish it in his newspaper, and the good citizens of Wallton will know that their children are now forever safe.

I wish you to know that I truly thank you for the few times we spent together at the bank, setting up the reward money. Only I knew it would never be collected.

George Eldridge Allen
September 22, 1933

After sitting at his desk for nearly an hour, Taylor telephoned Mason's office and indicated that, unless the doctor said it would be inconvenient, he would be at Mason's home late that evening.

"Tell him it's nothing urgent. Just want to show him something I got in the mail this morning. I probably won't get there until after he's had his supper, probably not until after ten o'clock."

It was closer to ten thirty when the doctor opened his door, and Taylor could tell that the man had been asleep. His hair was mussed, and he rubbed his eyes and the side of his face, trying to become fully awake.

"Must have dozed off for a minute," he apologized. "Come on in. Nights are really getting chilly now. Come over by the fire."

Taylor followed Mason into his parlor. He could not recall ever having been in that room before as the two usually sat in the kitchen. It was furnished nicely with a large hooked rug on the floor and white curtains with ruffled valances covering two windows. A leather sofa, a matching chair and a floor lamp were arranged in front of a fireplace, its mantel holding a vase and two framed photographs. He assumed that Mason was using the parlor that night because of the fireplace, its flames throwing shadows over the walls and ceiling.

"Late for a call, isn't it?"

"Yes, it is, Taylor agreed. "I know you're tired, but I wanted to give you this letter." Taylor handed the envelope over and continued. "I wanted you to see it. Don't think I will show it to anyone else. After you read it, give me your opinion."

Mason put on glasses and took some time reading and digesting the words. Finally he looked at Taylor, as though he couldn't believe what he saw written on the pages. Carefully he refolded the letter and returned it to its envelope.

"We were right. It was someone local."

"True, Doc, but I would never have thought about the banker . . . not in a million years."

"Nor would I," Mason responded. "He put up reward money. Why'd he do such a thing?"

"We'll never know for sure. I can only make a guess . . . that he felt remorse . . . or that he hoped he would be caught . . . stopped."

"Or he felt that offering the reward would make it seem very unlikely that he would be the killer," Mason interjected. "I know both you and I thought it was very nice of him to take so much interest in trying to find the individual killing the children. So good of him to offer such a large reward. Maybe it was simply to protect himself."

"That could be the reason," Taylor agreed. "As I said, I would never have considered him. He was our most upstanding citizen, the one who did so much for the community, all of the Christmas festivities . . . I prefer to believe that he put up the reward money because he felt so guilty . . . was in such turmoil over what he had done. It must have been terrible living with such a burden."

"Guess you could be right. After all, you may have known him better than most people in town. Course you only knew him slightly . . ."

"I didn't know him at all. That's obvious. I guess when you really come right down to it, no one knew him. His sister told me she didn't, and she'd lived with him all of those years."

"Good thing she's gone," Mason said. "Awful thing for her to have had to learn."

"Yes, but I think she knew all along. Just think it was too painful for her to admit to herself . . . to admit that the brother she loved . . . and I think she truly loved him . . . could kill anyone, especially small children."

Mason merely nodded, got up and put some more wood on the fire.

Taylor also stood.staring into the flames,and then smiled at the doctor. "Well, as Mr. Allen said in his letter, Wallton's parents won't have to worry any longer. Their kids are now safe."

After a few more minutes had elapsed, Mason walked the sheriff to the door. For a few seconds the two men merely stood silent, looking into each other's faces. Finally, Taylor smiled and said as he started out into the night, "Well, Doc. I may not be coming around quite as often as I have been. Really going to miss your cooking!"

CPSIA information can be obtained
at www.ICGtesting.com
Printed in the USA
BVHW030303040920
588090BV00001B/32